EDGE OF BETRAYAL

A DELIA CAHILL THRILLER

BY

CHUCK MORGAN

Printed in the United States of America

First printing 2025

ISBN 978-1-968179-33-5 (Paperback)

LIBRARY OF CONGRESS CONTROL NUMBER

2025912198

Table of Contents

Dedication

To the seekers of truth and the guardians of secrets,
    To those who walk the line between light and shadow,

    Who understand that courage is not the absence of
fear, but the will to press on despite it.

Paradise Interrupted

Delia Cahill tilted her glass toward the sun as if toasting its descent. The drink had grown warm in the Caribbean heat, melting into a swirl of sweet and sharp that pooled in the glass's belly. She took a sip, tasting mint and indecision, while waves whispered against the shore. The horizon with pinks and golds, painting a backdrop that didn't match the way she tensed when the secure phone rang beside her. Delia let it ring twice before answering. There were a handful of trusted people who had her number.

The voice, recognizable from the accent, came through as if he lounged beside her, imposing on the tranquility of the scene. Delia's body tensed, instinctively bracing for the undercurrent of authority in his words.

"How are you enjoying retirement?" he asked, like a father inquiring about a child's school day, though Delia understood that the conversation was anything but trivial.

Her gaze drifted to the outline of a yacht slicing through the horizon, its leisure an ironic contradiction to the tightening knot in her stomach as she clutched the glass.

"It's growing on me," she replied, her voice maintaining an airy façade. "Sunsets and mojitos have a certain charm. What can I do for you?"

She could almost picture his smirk, the kind that so often bordered on condescending, as he chuckled. The sound was familiar and unsettling, more calculated than amused. He didn't answer her question, and she was ready to disconnect the call.

"I hate to interrupt. A friend of mine has a situation."

Delia's grip tightened further, knuckles growing pale, as she leaned back against the lounge chair. Delia looked like a goddess. Her body was tanned dark from hours spent lying in the sun on her private beach. The ocean seemed to murmur in sympathy with the tension that enveloped her, each wave lapping at the shore with increasing insistence. She inhaled, holding on to the calm she had convinced herself was real. Had he made his next move, even before she had time to blink?

"I'm sure there's someone else qualified," she countered, forcing nonchalance into every syllable. "I don't work in that field anymore."

The words were easy, but the risks were not. She had left the Organization under a cloud, handed over her security credentials, her access codes and so much more, all because she had been betrayed by them. She had traded knives and pistols for sunsets and fruity cocktails.

She felt safe in her enclave, but she always worried about the new director of the Organization and his desire to track her down. She had killed his predecessor, and he was never one to let go of his assets easily. She had avoided outside work to remain safe. She hesitated, listening to the caller.

There was a pause, a calculated beat that hung heavy in the salt-tinged air. Delia held her breath, but he didn't leave the silence empty for long.

"This one needs your touch," he insisted, with a warmth that felt as manipulative as it was reassuring. "It's too delicate for just anyone."

Delia listened in silence, allowing him to fill in the gaps. It was a tactic she had learned from him long ago.

"A U.S. diplomat's son has been taken in Turkey. The Kahve Kodu was involved. We need your skills."

"I'm retired. Find someone else." Her response was immediate, her words clipped and defiant.

The caller paused, letting the silence draw out, a master at giving the illusion of choice.

"I know you are reluctant to come out of hiding, but this is important. Besides, you were requested by the child's father."

"Who is the father?" she asked.

"You'll be given all the information when you get to Istanbul," said the caller.

"How do you know I'll show?" she asked.

The caller laughed. "Delia Cahill has never walked away from a challenge, especially one involving a child. Do this job for me and I'll see if I can help you get your old friends off your back."

"You'll forgive me if I don't believe you. I was thinking about moving again anyway," she said.

"With the money you took from the terrorist after you stabbed him in his office, you are among the richest women in the world, and you can go anywhere you want, but I'm giving you a chance to not have to spend the rest of your life looking over your shoulder."

"Istanbul?" she asked.

"Istanbul. One of my people will contact you upon arrival. Safe travels." The line went dead, leaving the whisper of waves and the rustle of palm leaves.

Delia sat still, her body a study in contrast. Her relaxed position in the beach chair belied the tightness in her jaw and the way her hand gripped the glass until the ice shifted and cracked. She compelled herself to breathe, staring at the sunset with eyes that saw past the colors into a landscape of decisions and consequences.

The scene before her grew blurry, edges smudged by the unexpected tug of emotion she rarely let herself feel. Retirement was supposed to be a clean break. But like everything in her life, it was proving more complicated. She set the glass down, untouched since the call, and observed the waves roll in and out as if counting down her resolve. She liked it here, and she would hate to move.

Minutes passed, marked by the changing hues in the sky and her shifting posture as she weighed the threat against her instinct to defy. She replayed the conversation, analyzing each nuance in the caller's tone. Even though he was one of a handful of people she trusted, she still needed to be careful. In her line of work, alliances changed like the weather. The caller also knew that if he betrayed her, the consequences would be dire.

The soft breeze turned cooler, ruffling her auburn hair and drawing goose bumps along her arms. Delia took one last look at the ocean, now shadowed with dusk, and rose from the chair. Her actions were deliberate, each step a calculated surrender to the inevitable. She picked up her phone and dialed a number she thought she would never have to use again. The conversation was brief; she disconnected the call, finished her drink and headed for her bungalow.

Delia's footprints in the sand dissolved with the tide as if she had never been there at all. Inside, the beachfront bungalow glowed in the dimming light, shadows stretching like memories she couldn't quite leave behind. Her fingers brushed the walls and the furniture, each touch a silent farewell. When she got to the bedroom, her movements became methodical. She unearthed the go-bag from beneath a loose floorboard, its contents echoing a life she hadn't escaped after all. The room filled with weapons and whispers of betrayal, her meticulous packing interrupted by moments of longing she had tried to forget.

She moved through the bungalow, eyes scanning each room as if committing them to memory. The space was luxurious but minimal, signs of her long stay visible in the books on the shelves and the well-worn path from the bed to the window. A place meant for relaxation now felt like a cage closing in around her.

Delia unzipped the go bag, and the soft light illuminated the glint of metal as she spread its contents on the bed. The sleek silhouettes of weapons contrasted with the peaceful surroundings of the bungalow. Fingers moved with precision, securing each piece with an expert touch.

Her fingers ran over the smooth surfaces of her guns, tracing the familiar lines and curves. They moved as if they had a mind of their own. As she handled each weapon, she felt the weight and balance, knowing them intimately.

The faint scent of gun oil lingered. The familiar metallic tang of the weapons mixed with the subtle hint of leather from the bag itself. The room, once filled with the salty ocean breeze, now carried the sharp aroma of intrigue.

The pair of composite knives glinted in the light. Old friends who had never let her down. Delia studied them with a trained eye before placing them in their sheaths.

Next came the documents. Passports, currency and credentials. She flipped through them with the seasoned eye of someone who lived a hundred lives at once. Her polished exterior mirrored the tools of her trade, each as much a part of her as the other.

Her movements slowed when she got to the personal items. An unmailed letter addressed to David sat beside a stack of books. David didn't have an encrypted laptop, so she had to reach him by mail. It was a complicated process to keep her location secret even from him. She picked it up, the paper soft from repeated handling, yet never sent. She set it down, her touch lingering a moment too long before she continued.

The wedding photo was tucked into the corner of the mirror, its glossy surface dulled by dust. A thin film of neglect covered it, matching the layer of distance that had settled over her marriage. Delia hesitated, her hand hovering over the frame, as if touching it might dissolve the fragile world she had tried to create with David. With a reluctant breath, she turned it face up, staring at the image of herself and David, their smiles frozen in time. Her wedding dress was impossibly white against the shadows it now cast across her life, a sharp difference from the gray areas she inhabited.

On closer inspection, the photo revealed her own expression, a kind of tentative happiness that seemed foreign even then and misplaced now. Her smile, though bright, carried with it uncertainty, a flickering hope that had failed to become anything more lasting. It was a moment she had convinced herself could be real, captured on glossy paper but never quite substantial enough to endure. How long had it been face down, ignored like the promises she couldn't keep?

David's trust was as solid as ever; his smile unburdened by the secrets she carried. For an instant, her eyes filled with something she refused to name. She placed it back down, unable to look at it for more than a moment.

The image seemed to haunt her, even when it was not in her line of sight. She turned the photo face down again, as if doing so could bury the truth it held. The motion was as swift as removing a bandage, as if she needed it to be over to spare herself the pain of looking too closely.

Delia continued packing; the bag filled with the instruments of her dual existence. Each item seemed to accuse her, reminding her of a past she had pretended to leave. She slipped off her bikini, three small pieces of fabric that left nothing to the imagination. She looked at herself in the mirror.

Delia was gorgeous, tall and fit. Her tanned legs were long and sculpted, her abs were tight, and her breasts were large and firm, always straining against the fabric that confined them. Her long blond hair was gone, replaced with short dark auburn hair that glowed in the sunlight like fire.

She stepped into her shower and let the hot water wash over her. She covered her body in luxurious suds and thought about David. Her finger traced a line down the center of her abs, slid over a thin strip of blond hair and moved deep inside her. Her body tingled. She moved her finger until it found her pleasure spot, and she massaged it until she was ready. She reached through the lather and twisted one of her rock-hard nipples, and she exploded, screaming and leaning against the wall to keep from falling as her legs gave out. She slid down the wall, lay on the floor and let the water from the waterfall shower head wash over her. Her body shook.

Delia toweled off and dressed in her casual travel clothes: jeans and a T-shirt. She slipped on a pair of Nikes, picked up her go bag and walked to the door.

She stood at the doorway, taking one last look at the bungalow. The scene outside was idyllic, the ocean a silent witness to her return to the life she thought she had escaped. She hoped she would see it again. She shouldered the bag, familiar and unwelcome, before walking out into the night.

A Father's Desperation

Delia stepped into the safe house, the light dim and minimal. The building looked abandoned and in disarray, with dust covering the sparse furniture and cobwebs in the corners. The only light came from a single flickering bulb in the ceiling, casting an eerie glow over the muted room.

Delia's black clothing blended in with the shadows, making her appear like a phantom in the dim space. A faint musty odor hung in the air, likely from the old furniture and lack of ventilation. It mixed with the scent of old cigarettes and the distant fragrance of spice from the open-air market.

The clamor of the outside world sounded distant, the honking of cars blending into a muted buzz. Inside there was only the soft creak of floorboards beneath Delia's feet and the faint rustle of her hoodie as she shifted her weight.

She was dressed all in black, and the hoodie covered her hair. Her senses pricked, and she scanned the room as the sounds of the distant call to prayer mingled with the traffic outside. She saw him as soon as she entered. James Morrison, the special envoy with the United States State Department, was fifty years old, tall and trim, with silver hair. The last time she had seen him, many years ago, he had been immaculately dressed and looked debonair. The man standing before her was none of those things. His face was haggard and lined with exhaustion, his eyes sunken and shadowed with dark circles. His hair, usually well-groomed, was now disheveled and gray. His suit, once pristine, was now wrinkled and stained.

A single lamp exposed his fragility. James Morrison's hands shook as he paced the worn carpet. The space held a stained table where a coffee cup clinked like a small, persistent alarm. Delia paused, eyes narrowing, the mission already breathing down her neck.

Morrison turned toward her, his face gaunt and eyes bloodshot. Desperation etched lines across his forehead; his composure unraveled. The sight of him struck Delia with an unexpected pang, but she pushed it aside, reminding herself why she was there. She moved carefully, assessing him with the expertise she was known for. The room felt claustrophobic; the air filled with anticipation of what he was about to say.

"Please find my son." Morrison's voice was raw, scraping against the silence. It caught in the back of his throat, revealing more than the words themselves. "The official channels—it's like they're not even trying."

Delia studied him. He paced again, his hand running through his hair in a gesture of helplessness. She wondered why he had asked for her specifically. The first time they had met, she had been introduced to him as a high-powered attorney. Her clientele included some of the wealthiest, most powerful people in the world. She wondered what had changed.

Besides being an attorney to the rich and powerful, Delia Cahill was also an elite assassin. She wondered what Morrison knew about her alternate life. Her concern grew deep, and her senses went on high alert. She reached under her black windbreaker and touched the handles of her knives resting in their sheaths against her back. Knowing they were there gave her a feeling of control.

"They don't care. They're following protocol, wasting time." His anger flared, hot and brief, before it faded into despair. "I can't lose him. Not like this. Since his mother died, he's all I have left of her. Jennifer, my current wife, doesn't care about him. She won't lift a finger to help. The problem is that to give them what they want, I need her."

She considered him, weighing his words against the cold calculation of her training. "What have you heard?" she asked, her tone measured, neutral. It was a lawyer's question, one designed to extract information without revealing intent.

Morrison stopped, the stress in his body palpable. "They want something I can't give. Not without destroying everything I've worked my entire life for. It's something I shouldn't even have access to, but I can get it, and I don't know who I can trust."

"And what do you think that is?" Delia prompted, showing neither sympathy nor judgment. Her voice remained steady, a stark contrast to his trembling.

"They've gone dark. No communication for over twenty-four hours. I'm running out of time." His eyes pleaded with her, searching for something that would convince him she understood the costs. "I'm considering giving them classified information to get him back."

The words fell between them like a grenade. Morrison flinched at his own confession, the admission so raw it left him exposed. Delia held his gaze, her face betraying nothing, though the admission churned inside her.

"Do you know what you're saying?" she asked, each word weighted.

His silence answered for him. He looked away, the sheer weight of his situation crushing him from all sides. "I have to get him back," he repeated, softer now, the fight bleeding out of him.

Delia absorbed this, her instincts clashing with the fractured empathy she couldn't quite suppress. She knew the desperation of a man pushed to the edge, understood what it meant to compromise everything for the chance to save what you loved.

"The local police said it was a crime of opportunity," Morrison continued, trying to rationalize, to make sense of the chaos. "The embassy agreed with them. They said it happens all the time, and once they get a small ransom, they'll release him. But it's not. It's targeted. Planned. Somehow, they knew I had access. All anyone wants to do is wait for the kidnappers to make contact, but they already have. There will be no other contact until I am ready to give them what they want."

Delia's silence urged him on, allowing the truth to spill out.

"Every moment they do nothing is a moment he gets further away," Morrison said, his voice thick with anguish. He turned away and put his hands on his face. "I'm helpless here. You're the only one . . ."

The sentence dangled, lost in despair, the unspoken words more telling than if he had pleaded aloud: the only one I trust. The only one who might care. The implication pressed on her, pushing at the walls of the small room, echoing in the silence that followed. He covered his face with his hands.

Delia remained where she stood, arms crossed, her mind working, calculating the risk. "What makes you think I can help?" she asked, her voice measured but with an edge that betrayed her uncertainty. She was torn between the mission and the man, his desperation an unwelcome reminder of things she preferred to keep buried.

Morrison looked up at her, a glimmer of hope breaking through his desolation. His eyes were wet with tears, with the vulnerability she had long since trained herself to hide.

"I was told that you have certain skills that might be useful in this situation." His words were a lifeline, cast out in her direction, a last effort to reach her, to make her see what was at stake.

Delia's eyes narrowed, her mind clicking over the possibilities. She knew her reputation was flawless, unassailable. But it was also supposed to be secret.

"Who gave you that information?" she asked, each word primed with a soft, professional veneer that disguised the danger beneath.

Her inquiry was sharp, designed to cut through the veils, to reveal the leak. She had to know how deep this had already gone.

Morrison hesitated, the pressure of her question pressing down on him. He seemed to fold under its intensity, his eyes filled with all the fear and urgency he could not contain. He swallowed hard and stared at her again, his expression as much a question as it was an answer.

"I'm desperate, and I was told you're the best."

"Don't flatter me, James," said Delia, sharper than she meant for it to come out. "Who?"

James Morrison did not answer right away. He seemed, in that moment, as old as the worn carpet, his voice stripped of all the careful, stately polish of a diplomat and father.

"Years ago," he said, the words bitter as a bad cup of coffee, "I was with the agency. No one knows that. I went through the farm like anyone else, but after my first field tour I was transferred. State claimed me, and that was that. I was a diplomat, a man for the soft sell." He let out a short, humorless laugh. "You know how that is, Delia. They never want the real story. Only what fits their narrative."

He paced between the battered table and the gray radiator, collecting his thoughts. Delia glanced at him, measuring the old man against her memory of the one she'd met before. She remembered the dinner in Vienna, a table set with white linen, Morrison laughing at some joke about the Hungarian ambassador's wife, everyone pretending not to know what the others did in their off-hours.

"I never told anyone about this," Morrison continued, now speaking to the wall. "Not even Jennifer. Especially not Jennifer. But it was ten years ago, maybe more. The op was here in Istanbul—a weapons dealer, ex-KGB, went by the name Belinsky. He was on a short list for acquiring a nuclear device. At least, that's what Langley thought."

His hands were open, gesturing helplessly. "Everyone thought he was untouchable. We had nothing. The guy was a ghost. They said our only play was to blackmail a Turkish asset, but the station chief balked." He pivoted and looked her in the eye for the first time since she'd entered.

"Somebody up the chain called in the Organization. The director at the time was old-school, a real bastard, but he got results.

"The director told me an asset would be assigned. I'd never meet them, never knew a name, never asked questions, just facilitated. I did what I was told. No one wanted a black mark on their career, not with something like that hanging over us. The last thing I heard was the job was done. The bodies were retrieved by Turkish Intelligence and disappeared. It was like Belinsky never existed."

Delia remembered the target, though she couldn't have attached a name to the face if pressed. She knew it had rained as she followed the target and his bodyguard through the crowd. The way the bodyguard noticed the stranger in the crowd. He had moved to intercept but was not fast enough, and he died for his efforts. She thought back on the soft slip of metal, the wet gurgle, the splatter. There had been a moment of quiet after, as if the city held its breath before the screaming and chaos began. And then the job was done. No questions, no loose ends.

Morrison wiped a hand across his cheek, and she registered the smallest tremor, the way his fingers hesitated at the memory.

"I only found out years later. The director reached out to me for a favor; State had something he wanted. I made it happen. We had dinner one evening, and the conversation turned to the op in Istanbul. After a few glasses of wine, he told me who you were. He was proud of you, like a father would be of a daughter. He said there was nobody better." Morrison looked down at the floor, as if ashamed of what he'd done. "If you're worried about security, about exposure, I swear to you, Delia, no one knows but me. I would stake my life on that."

Another silence, longer this time. Morrison poured himself another cup of coffee and sat on the battered couch. The mug rattled against the saucer, his hands unsteady.

"When Tommy was taken, I didn't trust the local authorities. The embassy is useless, and the bureau sent some junior G-man who doesn't know his ass from a hole in the ground. There's nobody else I can turn to. I reached out to someone I trust, someone outside the government. He said you were retired." His voice broke, and he steadied it, gripping the mug like a lifeline. "Money is no object. I just want my son back. I don't care what it takes. I need you."

Delia let this all settle, the heaviness pressing down on her shoulders. She'd been in rooms like this before, dozens, maybe hundreds. The faces and the stories changed, but the desperation, the quiet panic underneath, was always the same. It was why people like Morrison eventually came to people like her.

She thought back to Belinsky, to the countless other jobs that had passed through her hands. The target in Istanbul was just a blip, one of many that had been erased from the world so thoroughly their existence became rumor.

She looked at him, her hard edges softening just enough to let a trace of humanity show through. She was pissed that the previous director would expose her to an outsider. This was troubling.

"What will you do?" His question was a plea, stripping away the last of his defenses.

Delia hesitated, her own barriers eroding in the face of his naked vulnerability. The impulse to protect battled with years of conditioning, a silent war waged in the slight tremor of her hands.

When she spoke, her voice was low but firm. "I'll find your son." The promise felt like both a burden and a release, tying her to a mission she wouldn't walk away from.

Morrison sagged with relief, the fight leaving him like a punctured tire. "Thank you," he whispered, the words thick with gratitude and fear. He sank into a chair, the adrenaline that had kept him upright dissipating now that she had committed. "I will wire the funds to any account you want."

"I want one thing from you, James. Do not give up any of our government's secrets."

Delia turned her attention to the picture he held in his hand. The photo of Tommy drew her eye: a smiling boy with tousled hair and innocent eyes. The image struck her like a blow, his vulnerability mirroring a past she had spent a lifetime escaping. She held the picture, a simple gesture that betrayed the depth of her empathy. The boy's trusting face burned into her mind. Then she pulled back, her mask of professional detachment sliding into place as she prepared to leave.

"I won't let you down," she said, the conviction in her voice surprising them both. It was more than a promise; it was a vow that bound her to a cause she understood all too well.

Morrison met her gaze, his eyes a battlefield of hope and despair. Delia felt the responsibility of his trust settle onto her shoulders, lessening his burden but increasing hers.

"What about the Organization? I heard you left under a cloud. Can you do this and protect yourself?" His question wavered between belief and doubt, seeking the certainty he needed to cling to.

"I can." Her response was immediate, as much a reassurance for herself as for him. "I can."

His posture changed, his back straightening as the first flicker of genuine relief crossed his features. He rubbed a hand over his face, the gesture clearing away some of the shadows beneath his eyes.

"You have no idea what this means," he said.

Delia gazed at him, her heart pulling her towards a resolution that felt dangerous in its familiarity. "Yes, I do." The words carried the weight of personal history, an understanding she couldn't suppress even if she wanted to.

His gaze fell upon her, a man clawing back from the edge. "If there's anything, anything at all you need from me . . ."

"Just hold on." The simplicity of her answer masked the complexity of the task ahead. "I'll be in touch."

Morrison's gratitude was palpable, filling the room with a warmth that pushed back the shadows, the weariness of days without sleep catching up to him now that he had something to believe in.

"Thank you," he murmured again, the words so full of emotion they almost collapsed under their own weight.

Delia took a last look around. The dim light cast Tommy's photo in stark relief, the boy's face innocent and unknowing. It spurred her on. The empathy she felt for the boy, and perhaps for herself, didn't weaken her. It gave her purpose.

Her mind raced with plans, strategies knitting together in the space between her breaths. She stood, shouldering the full measure of the promise she had made. The photo's image seared itself into her memory, a beacon guiding her resolve.

Morrison stared at her, his eyes following her every move. The mixture of hope and trust on his face was an unspoken plea and an indication of his faith in her. It pushed her forward, each step she took from the table, an obligation she now carried.

She arrived at the door, her hand pausing on the knob as she took one last look back. Morrison was alone, the silence wrapping around him like a shroud now that her presence no longer filled the room. The vulnerability she saw in him strengthened her resolve.

Delia stepped outside, the night air cool and invigorating, like a shot of adrenaline to her system. The door clicked shut behind her, the sound final yet freeing. She was already immersed in the task, strategies spinning into a web of determination and risk.

The dark street stretched out before her, dim lights tracing her silhouette as she walked away. Each step echoed with purpose, her focus narrowing to the singular goal of rescuing Tommy and unraveling the truth behind his kidnapping.

Morrison's words, Tommy's photo, her own haunted past—they blurred together, fueling her drive. She pulled up her hood and disappeared into the night.

Shadows of Conspiracy

Delia crossed the street, her reflection slipping over office windows like a ghost. The building looked unremarkable, a gray façade in a commercial district, but she knew better. Inside, the government's pulse quickened through a labyrinth of surveillance and security. She breezed past the front desk, a visitor expected yet unwelcome.

Hidden cameras followed her progress, scrutinizing her every step. When she walked into the conference room, her contact rose to greet her. His tailored suit projected control, but the shadows beneath his eyes hinted at the perils.

"This isn't a random kidnapping," he said, gauging her reaction with surgical precision.

She remained unreadable, eyes steady as she absorbed the statement. "That's not a surprise," she replied, her voice carrying an edge that cut through the sterile air. The room was like a stage, one she had performed on many times, but this act held more gravity than usual.

Her contact, Hamza Demir, motioned for her to sit, his movements measured. Hamza was a dignified-looking man with silver hair and a gray goatee. He wore an expensive custom-made suit and silk tie, a sign of good breeding. He had gained a little weight around the middle since the last time she had seen him, but he still looked fit. She knew he still trained like the ex–military officer he was.

"They knew who to target and when," he continued, leaning over with his fingers steepled. The intensity of his gaze suggested layers of meaning behind each word.

Delia settled into the chair, its hard surface and straight-backed design offering no comfort. She crossed her legs and arms in a posture of practiced defiance.

"And how did they manage that?" she asked, challenging him with her directness.

He allowed a slight pause, the kind that tested patience. "We've seen indications of a breach," he admitted, his voice low and resonant. "A troubling one."

She studied him, weighing the admission. The dynamic between them crackled with the familiarity of two chess players contemplating their next moves. Her silence pushed him to fill the gap.

"Are you guys spying on the U.S. Embassy?" she asked, a smile on her face.

Hamza laughed. "Of course not. Don't you read the news on the internet? Our countries are friends, remember? The whole NATO thing."

Delia cocked her head to one side and looked at him. "So, what do you know?"

"Morrison's access to classified stealth fighter plans made his son a valuable target," Hamza elaborated. "They approached this with military precision."

"So, trained operatives. Any idea who they work for?" Delia asked, her eyes narrowing.

The statement hung between them, charged with implication. She leaned back, maintaining her composure despite the jolt of adrenaline the conversation sparked.

"Initial information says the Kahve Kodu are involved," Hamza said, the name itself a subtle test to see if she would flinch.

He adjusted his cuff links with a movement that looked practiced, but Delia noted the faint tremor in his left hand. Hamza didn't get nervous easily, and he certainly didn't show it if he did.

Delia sifted the phrase through her mind. Kahve Kodu, the Coffee Code. Istanbul's most intricate, least understood criminal syndicate, built on layers of tradition, subterfuge and currency that had nothing to do with lira. They were myth and rumor, a shadow society woven through teahouses and dockyards, with roots older than the Republic itself. Delia had heard the name before in briefings that read like urban legends, and in whispers by agency handlers who regarded their methods with a mixture of awe and dread.

"You're not dealing with professionals," Hamza continued, though the words sounded like an undermining, deliberate misdirection.

"Kahve Kodu runs the waterfront, sure, but they're more dockworkers than black ops. Smuggling, loan-sharking, the occasional score. They aren't known for this level of sophistication."

Delia considered this. If the Kahve Kodu had really snatched Morrison's kid, it meant one of two things. Either someone on the inside was moonlighting or the syndicate had evolved in ways not even the local authorities understood.

She pressed: "Then why does this feel so tightly wound? No ransom, no message. Who takes a diplomat's son and stays silent?"

Hamza's eyes flickered, an admission of uncertainty. "It doesn't fit their pattern," he conceded. "But their fingerprints are all over the logistics. The abduction point, the vehicle dump site, even the burner phone traces all point to Kahve Kodu territory."

The memory of the crime scene flickered in her mind: the abandoned sedan with its doors open to the rain, a child's backpack left as a decoy. It was orchestrated, but not in the way Western syndicates operated.

She leaned forward, voice low. "Maybe they're subcontracting. Or maybe someone's using their network as cover."

Hamza shook his head slightly, as if to clear away the fog of half-baked theories. "The boss, the so-called Patron, is a ghost. We have no leverage with him. If they're being used, it's by a player we haven't even identified."

The silence in the room deepened, broken only by the hum of recycled office air. Delia remembered what the director had told her years ago: "Istanbul is a city where every truth wears a different costume by sunset." This was feeling like one of those truths, layered, elusive and designed to keep her boxed in until she made a mistake.

Hamza finally broke the silence. "You want my advice? Don't trust anyone inside the embassy. We intercepted chatter that suggests this was in motion for weeks, maybe months."

Delia mapped the scenario in her mind: a diplomat's child caught between rival intelligence services, hired muscle doubling as pawns in a bigger game and a local syndicate with roots too deep to pull. She sensed the old spark of anticipation, the sense that came before every operation: when the pieces moved, but you weren't yet sure if you were playing the game or being played.

The words hung in the air. Delia was walking into a complex web, the strands already beginning to twist around her. Hamza watched her closely, his expression revealing nothing but the gravity of the situation.

Her gaze shifted around the room, taking in the sterile environment with its high-tech displays and the old-fashioned paper files marked classified that sat in neat piles. The juxtaposition was striking, proof of the multifaceted nature of the world she used to operate in.

The walls were bare, the space designed for function over form. Yet the austere setting spoke volumes. Each element meticulously conveyed both transparency and secrecy. Delia noted it all with a critical eye. She understood the language of power.

Hamza waited, allowing her time to absorb the surroundings and the importance of his words. His patience was measured, an unspoken challenge to see who would break the silence first.

"You're certain the leak is internal?" Delia asked, her voice sharp and probing. Her skepticism was palpable, a force she wielded like a weapon.

"We have strong reasons to believe so," he replied. His brown eyes met hers, steady and unwavering. "The timing and the nature of the information point to a well-placed source in the embassy."

Delia nodded, her expression giving away little. But inside, her mind worked furiously, assembling the pieces of a puzzle that seemed more complex with each revelation. The familiar thrill of uncertainty mingled with the risk of betrayal, a combination she understood all too well.

"You brought me in to find Tommy," she said, letting the boy's name hang between them with intentional weight. Her words were more statement than question, asserting her role in the unfolding drama.

"Yes," he affirmed, leaning back with an air of practiced authority. "Your expertise is crucial, if we hope to retrieve him without compromising U.S. national security."

Her presence in the room had been expected, but now it was essential. Hamza's expression remained composed, yet his eyes hinted at the ramifications. Delia registered it all.

Their eyes locked, each sizing up the other in a silent battle of wills. The familiar tug of duty and danger washed over her, a lure she could never resist. She had walked into this knowing the risks, but the undertaking was weighing on her.

"This isn't a game, Delia," he cautioned, his voice carrying an undercurrent of something that might have been concern. "The players are ruthless, the consequences are real and you've been out of the game for quite a while."

"I know what I'm doing," she countered, the conviction in her voice unshakable.

The statement was as much for herself as it was for him. She understood the terrain she was navigating, even if it shifted beneath her feet.

Hamza observed her with the patience of someone accustomed to getting his way, yet he also understood the tenacity of the woman before him. She had trained too well for him to expect blind obedience.

"Then you understand the urgency, and you need to be at the top of your game," he said, a note of finality in his tone. "Tommy Morrison's life depends on it."

Hamza led Delia to a room deeper in the bowels of the building. He placed his face up to a wall-mounted screen, and a red line scanned his face. The door clicked, and he pulled it open. He held the door so Delia could pass through first. She sat at the large conference table. Glowing screens covered one wall, filled with surveillance photos and intelligence reports weaving a tale of power and betrayal. Hamza moved with calm authority, narrating the story in measured tones. Delia eyed him, her instincts tingling as he glossed over crucial details. The omissions were deliberate, glaring. Her patience frayed. She rose, her sudden movement slicing the air with unspoken defiance.

"How about we stop fucking around? I'm not walking into this blind," she declared, each word a challenge.

Hamza hesitated; his jaw tightened, and she recognized the tell. "Some of this is highly sensitive," he said, conceding ground.

He leaned over the console, images flickering in rapid succession as his words painted a dangerous landscape. "This syndicate isn't new to us. They've been expanding aggressively," he explained, tapping a few keys. "Turkey, Eastern Europe, the Middle East. Wherever there's chaos, they're there."

Delia sat and followed the shifting visuals, her gaze as precise as her questions. "And the gaps? They just appear out of thin air?"

Hamza straightened, smoothing the front of his suit with practiced ease. "We've traced several known associates," he continued, dodging the inquiry. "Each plays a critical role in the network."

The photos changed again, but Delia noticed how he sidestepped, skipping files she was sure existed. Her patience thinned with every curated slide.

He seemed unfazed, maintaining a rhythm of control and deflection. "The Kahve Kodu's been busy," he noted, pointing to a grainy image. "Most of their recent activities center around this man, Edip Batir."

Delia saw through his tactics. He was holding back, filtering her access with the exactness of a master puppeteer. Her instincts screamed for more.

"What about their links to arms dealers?" she pressed, pushing him towards territory he wanted to avoid.

He hesitated, just enough for her to notice. "There's speculation," he said, the words measured and clipped.

Her eyes narrowed, catching every nuance in his posture and speech. Hamza continued to circle the elephant in the room, leaving her in the dark about key players.

Delia's frustration grew, simmering beneath her controlled exterior. She had danced this dance before, but never with so much at stake.

"Speculation won't help me out there," she countered, her voice sharper than she'd expected. "I'm seeing several blanks in your story."

He paused, letting the silence punctuate her accusation. He stepped from the console, giving her a long, deliberate look. "We're working on a need-to-know basis," he replied, the authority in his voice absolute.

She read the challenge in his words, recognizing his attempt to assert control. But this time, she wasn't playing by his rules.

Delia stood abruptly, the chair scraping against the floor as she pushed it back. Her hands planted firmly on the table.

"Either I get full disclosure, or I walk and you can explain to your friend Morrison why," she stated, her tone brooking no argument.

Hamza studied her, the tension thick. Their history stretched between them like a coiled spring, and she knew he understood the intensity of her commitment.

He leaned back, fingers drumming the table with infuriating calm. Delia watched him, refusing to relent. She had forced his hand before, and she would do it again.

The seconds ticked by, each one a battle of wills. He sighed, the sound more resigned than she expected. He pressed a button on the console, and the screens shifted to reveal hidden files.

Her persistence had paid off, but he made sure she understood the cost. "Some of this information is sensitive," he warned, the concession reluctant but unmistakable. "It doesn't leave this room."

Delia sat back down, her eyes devouring the new data. The omissions were no longer glaring, but the risk was even more apparent.

Hamza's jaw tightened, a subtle tell that spoke volumes. He'd lost this round, but the odds were still stacked in his favor.

"Thank you," she said, the words carrying both gratitude and triumph. She dove into the expanded intel, knowing full well the magnitude of what she'd uncovered. The files were a trove of potential and peril, each a thread she had to unravel.

Hamza's words were surgical strikes, precise and piercing. "Their reach extends into foreign intelligence services," he continued, his voice sharpening. "Your embassy and the Turkish government."

Delia absorbed the revelation, understanding the vast network they faced. A new image appeared on the screen. The photo showed a man built like a tank, his expression hard and unforgiving.

"Gerhardt Blume," he identified. "He's the middleman."

The consequences climbed higher, and Delia accepted their weight. This wasn't a mission. It was a minefield. She had to prepare for war if she was to get Tommy Morrison back.

The words and images pressed down on her. The syndicate's web was more intricate than she had imagined, strands reaching into places even Hamza seemed wary to touch.

"This isn't a small-time operation," he emphasized, his gaze as penetrating as his intel. "If the stealth fighter plans get into Blume's hands, our American friends won't be able to contain the fallout."

Delia understood his warning. She had seen the chaos a single leak could unleash. But this was bigger. Much bigger.

Hamza walked her through the implications with unerring clarity, his voice steady and sure. "The players involved are well-funded and relentless. Their connections run deeper than we expected. No one knows who can be trusted. It's like we are all flying in the dark without instruments."

Each statement was a blow, but Delia absorbed them with the resilience he expected from her. The risks were enormous, yet the challenge of the mission drew her in.

"We suspect some of their backing comes from sources within allied nations," he added, watching her for any sign of hesitation.

But Delia gave him none. She thrived on this kind of high-stakes uncertainty, even as it threatened to consume her.

He studied her, a glimmer of something like admiration crossing his features. "This is more than just a rescue," he acknowledged, validating the immense size of the task. "It's an international crisis."

Delia nodded, her focus razor-sharp as she connected the dots. Every revelation added a layer of urgency.

The photos shifted again, pausing on a candid shot of a man surrounded by luxury. Delia took in his stocky build, the blond hair and green eyes, the aura of danger.

"Blume," she repeated, imprinting every detail into her mind. His role was clear, and so was the peril.

"He's brokered similar deals before," Hamza continued, his words like a dossier coming to life. "But never on this scale. Our intel suggests he's in Turkey, orchestrating the operation. We are concerned that the plans for the stealth fighter are a part of a larger operation. One we have not fully grasped."

Delia listened, the intensity of her concentration evident in the way she leaned forward. She memorized Blume's habits, his known associates, any piece of data that might prove critical.

"He won't hold on to them for long," Hamza cautioned. "Once he gets them, he'll auction them to the highest bidder."

The sense of urgency tightened its grip. Delia was racing against a clock with too many hands.

Hamza placed a secure tablet in front of her, the device holding a comprehensive dossier of the syndicate's recent activities. "Everything you need is here," he said. "Six months of surveillance, communication intercepts, asset reports."

She reached for it, the information thrilling and daunting. This was her arsenal, her map through enemy territory.

As she held the tablet, his voice dropped lower, his next words heavier than the ones before. "There's something else you need to know," he admitted, reluctant but resolute. Delia looked up, catching the seriousness in his eyes. "We believe there's a mole."

The impact of the statement was immediate, its implications explosive. She processed it with the speed and skill of someone trained to expect betrayal at every turn.

"How high?" she asked, the question direct and dangerous.

Hamza's expression was neutral, a mask she knew well. "High enough to know the movements of top assets. High enough to stay one step ahead."

The suspicion hung between them, a live wire waiting to spark. It didn't change the facts, but it made her job tougher.

"That's what you need to find out," he said, each word deliberate and heavy.

Delia absorbed the challenge, aware of the shit storm she was about to walk into. This wasn't just about rescuing Tommy. It was about uncovering a conspiracy that reached into the heart of power.

Her eyes locked onto his, a moment of understanding passing between them. They were both deep in this game, but she was the one with her life on the line.

Hamza leaned back, his parting words a reminder and a warning. "Trust no one, not even your own people."

The seriousness of his statement resonated through her. Delia accepted the dangers of misplaced trust, and she wouldn't be caught off guard.

She rose to leave, the tablet secured and the mission clear. Each step was a step towards the unknown.

The sterile environment that had been stifling now buzzed with the thrill of what lay ahead. Delia experienced the familiar rush of adrenaline, the challenge both daunting and exhilarating.

"I'll be in touch," she said, the promise lingering like an unspoken agreement. Her eyes met Hamza's one last time, and she saw something almost paternal in his gaze.

"I will help you if I can, but I am limited in what I can do. Be careful, Delia, and remember that nothing in Istanbul is as it seems."

As she exited the building, the magnitude of the mission loomed large, but her resolve was unshakable. She would navigate this web of danger and deception. She would find the truth. As the door closed behind her, the sterile environment receded, but Hamza's words remained.

Outside, the world seemed unchanged, indifferent to the secrets and dangers she carried with her. Delia's pace quickened as she moved down the street, the determination in her step mirrored by the rapid pulse of the city around her.

She was unsure of where this mission was headed, but one thing was for certain. No matter what happened, she would bring Tommy home.

Istanbul Underworld

The crush of the city overwhelmed her, crowds pressing in from every direction. It was all she could do to keep a brisk pace. The Grand Bazaar loomed ahead, a colorful snare of tourists and stalls. There, Kemal would be waiting. Delia wore dark sunglasses and a scarf, her attire equal parts disguise and distraction. The rattle of a tram made her flinch, reminding her of her vulnerability. She gripped her backpack, ignoring her dry throat.

She plunged into the bazaar, a warren of colors and noise that seemed to close in from every direction. Stalls teemed with textiles, spices, jewelry. Vendors shouted, haggling with tourists who thronged the narrow alleys like schools of fish. The chaos threatened to sweep her up, but Delia fought to keep her focus. Her eyes scanned the rows of goods, lingering on the faces that passed, searching for Kemal among the crush of bodies.

The city had its own rhythm, its pulse loud and insistent. It thrummed through the marketplace, a constant beat that made her hyperaware of the life she'd left behind. Everything here seemed raw, vibrant, but she couldn't let herself get lost in it. Her senses had to stay sharp. Istanbul was nothing like the clinical world she was used to. It was alive with the very things she'd spent years trying to avoid.

Delia moved through the crowd, a solitary figure of intent amid the chaotic bustle. Roasted chestnuts and strong coffee permeated the air, mixing with the heat and dust until it was almost suffocating. She carefully adjusted her headscarf, ensuring her identity remained concealed as she navigated farther into the central area of the bazaar. Her pace was steady but quick, each step rehearsed to avoid attracting too much attention.

When she spotted the carpet stall, her shoulders tensed with recognition. Kemal leaned over his wares, gesturing with one hand and scratching his chin with the other. He had not aged well since the last time she saw him. His age showed in the deep lines of his face, his eyes narrowed as if he'd spent too many years staring into the sun. He didn't seem to see her at first, too focused on his act as a vendor uninterested in her arrival. But Delia knew he was aware. He always was.

She approached, feigning interest in the colorful rugs as she drew closer. The surrounding sound dimmed, the noise and chaos falling away until there was nothing but her and Kemal. He didn't look at her, his attention fixed on the handcrafted carpet in his hands.

"Nice work," Delia said, as if admiring the weave.

Kemal snorted, glancing her way. "You Americans and your tastes," he replied, his accent thick and his tone dismissive. But there was a glint in his eye, a signal they both understood. "It is good to see you again, my friend. It has been too many years since last we spoke. You have what I asked for?"

Delia slid the backpack towards him, her movement so subtle it could have gone unnoticed. He reached for it, still holding the colorful carpet in his other hand.

She watched his fingers as they lingered on the latch. "And you?" she asked, her words casual but weighted.

Kemal nodded, his face set in a grim line. "The docks," he murmured, eyes scanning the crowd, his focus never staying in one place too long. "But it's risky. Things have changed."

Delia read the hesitation in his stance, the doubt. "I can handle risk," she replied, her voice clipped, disguising any hint of the fear that edged her.

Kemal's squint deepened, skeptical. "Maybe. But these people . . . they are different. Dangerous."

"I am dangerous too," Delia said, the confidence forced but necessary.

"I hope you are dangerous enough," he said. He smiled, his teeth stained brown from years of smoking and strong coffee.

Their conversation lasted seconds, yet each word felt like an eternity. When he turned his attention to the carpet, it was a signal that their exchange was done. Delia hesitated, her instincts screaming caution, but she refused to second-guess herself. The bazaar swallowed her once again as she left the stall, her mind already sorting through Kemal's information.

She blended back into the throng, more a shadow than a person, her every step measured. There were eyes everywhere; she had to believe some of them were on her. The mission was taking shape, its complexity more than she had imagined, and the danger now had a location. But Kemal's warning plagued her. "They are different. Dangerous." His reluctance to give her more intel felt like an itch she couldn't scratch.

As she made her way towards the exit, Delia's attention never wavered. Her thoughts raced, but her focus remained absolute. She was never more than a stone's throw from the threat of exposure, the possibility that she had been recognized despite her precautions. Each passerby was a potential tail, each glance a question she didn't have time to answer. But she moved with the sharpness of a person who had survived this before and would again.

The weapon concealed beneath her jacket was a familiar comfort. She brushed it with her fingertips, an anchor to who she was and what she had to do. The feeling reminded her that she was far from helpless, that she could control this if she stayed sharp. If she stayed herself.

The noise from the bazaar faded as Delia reached the perimeter of the market. She cast a last look over her shoulder, her senses attuned to anything out of place. A couple of tourists argued over a price, an old man hawked fake leather goods and the world continued its relentless motion. Her pulse slowed, the adrenaline bleeding away as she merged into the currents of the street.

Her steps were brisk, confident, even as her mind continued to analyze Kemal's sparse intel. It was enough to set her on a path, but the shadows of uncertainty clung to it. She couldn't shake the feeling that he was hiding something. The syndicate was a larger beast than she had been led to believe. Delia would have to dig deeper, faster, before the trail went cold. Or before it consumed her.

She pushed ahead, vanishing into the sprawling city. Each stride marked a beat in the new and dangerous rhythm that would guide her.

Delia slipped into the shadows, becoming someone else. Black fabric hugged her form, and makeup transformed her features into the face of a stranger. Night swallowed Istanbul, turning the waterfront into a seedy warren. Red neon lights marked the Crimson Crescent, the club a known haunt for arms dealers and thugs.

Delia walked with the confidence of a woman who'd done this before, the fake ID like a skeleton key in her pocket. Music thudded through her bones as she entered, and the air was thick with smoke and desperation. She threaded through the crowd, always vigilant.

The bouncers barely glanced at her. She was just another face in the stream of people pushing their way inside. Once she was past the door, the noise enveloped her in an oppressive, rhythmic hug. Lights flashed like warnings, and the heat from packed bodies made the space feel more like a pressure cooker than a nightclub.

Delia surveyed the room, taking it all in with quick, deliberate glances. Criminals, corrupt officials and women selling more than drinks filled the club, each with their own agenda. She was just another shadow, but she knew better than to believe she went unnoticed. Several men had taken notice of her, and she hoped the extra makeup on top of the deep bronze tan would be enough to make her look like a local.

The bar ran along one side of the cavernous space, its surface gleaming with spilled liquor and half-finished drinks. Delia leaned against it. Her eyes continued their inventory. The noise was suffocating, and the constant thrum of bass seemed to vibrate in time with her pulse.

A couple near the entrance argued, their words lost in the din but their body language unmistakable. A young man sat slumped over a table, his glass precariously close to tipping. Everywhere she looked, deals were being made, whispers traded, power negotiated.

She left the bar, slipping back into the throng of bodies that crowded the dance floor. Her passage was fluid, like water finding the easiest route. She didn't have much time. If the intel was good, she had to be gone before anyone realized she was there.

Delia's gaze fixed on a booth at the far end of the club. Two men leaned close, their conversation meant for no one else. She changed direction, angling her way towards them with the tactical ease of someone who made a living on other people's secrets.

One man, blond and blue-eyed, wore a pale suit, poorly fitted, the fabric almost glowing in the dim light. He spoke with a German accent. The other, wearing jeans, a sweat-stained T-shirt and leather sandals, had dark hair and a scruffy beard. His shirt was stretched and misshapen at the collar. He looked like a typical dockworker, but the rest of his appearance spoke of control and refinement.

There was tension in their postures, a kind that spoke of deals and risk. She settled near them, close enough to watch without being intrusive, yet far enough to feign disinterest if anyone looked her way.

A passing server caught her attention, and she ordered a drink she didn't intend to touch. The server returned with her drink, and she handed him cash. Enough to keep him happy, but not enough to draw attention to herself. The glass stayed on the table, beads of condensation forming and pooling, forgotten. She leaned back in her chair, letting her eyes drift over the crowd while her focus remained on the men.

Their body language shifted as the conversation became more animated. Delia caught bits and pieces, enough to make her pulse quicken. They mentioned delivery dates, payments, the words sharp and metallic like bullets.

One leaned back, crossing his arms with a confidence that bordered on arrogance. The blond with the beard rubbed his chin, a gesture more anxious than he intended. Delia studied them, her instincts telling her this was bigger than even Hamza imagined.

The sounds of the club faded, the pulse of the music retreating until it was just background noise. The men's conversation was all she heard, the snippets falling into place like a map she was drawing from memory.

"It's a big score," the man in the pale suit said, his accent light and almost cheerful. "No one else is even close." Their voices floated over the noise, tight and hushed.

"A big score, huh," replied the bearded man. "What about the military tech?" His lined face and confident manner belied the tension in his voice.

The other man looked serious. "There are security protocols that must be followed," he murmured. Delia's pulse quickened. She strained to hear more.

The bearded man hesitated, looking around to ensure no one was eavesdropping. Delia held her breath, the thrill of discovery a live wire inside her.

"I'm still concerned about the diplomat's cooperation," he replied. His tone was a combination of worry and calculation.

Delia's heart raced. They knew about Morrison. This was confirmation she hadn't expected so soon.

She leaned in, her ears straining for more. But just as the next words left his mouth, the chaos she dreaded erupted around her.

Gunshots split the air, a jarring difference from the steady beat of the music. Delia's head snapped towards the entrance, where masked figures in black shoved past the bouncers with deadly intent. Panic spread like wildfire, the crowd devolving into a mass of bodies pushing and shouting.

It took seconds for the panic to reach her. The men's conversation fractured, lost to the rising chaos as the nightclub exploded into motion. Delia pivoted, her instincts taking over. The patrons shoved and shouted, their fear tangible, a living thing that threatened to crush her under its weight. She pushed through the mass of bodies, knowing the real danger was yet to come.

The armed men burst through the entrance, relentless in their advance. Delia caught sight of one, his face covered by a mask as he scanned the crowd. They were aware of who they were looking for. She had seconds, maybe less, to disappear before she was a target.

Delia didn't wait to see what would happen next. She was already on her feet, already moving, the impulse to survive outweighing the desire to know more. The men in the booth ducked behind the table, their conversation forgotten in the storm of violence that descended on the club.

Delia ran, her path an improvised dance through the tangle of panicked patrons. Her mind computed a dozen routes, narrowing down to the most direct escape. The back of the club loomed ahead, a glowing exit sign like a beacon in the chaos. She made for it, every step a desperate play to outrun the syndicate's reach.

She barreled through the kitchen, an island of order that devolved into pandemonium. She grabbed the tray, yanking it from a server's hands and sending its contents crashing to the floor. Dishes shattered, and the staff's confusion splintered any attempt at pursuit. She bolted through the service door and into the alley.

The air outside was cool and filled with cooking aromas, and Delia looked for the fastest way out. She spotted a large group of people at one end of the alley, and she headed that way. She didn't slow, her feet finding purchase on the slick pavement, and she bolted into the narrow alleys that snaked through Istanbul's darkened streets. Her breath came in quick bursts, adrenaline fueling her flight.

She hit a dark corner, and an enormous beast of a man stepped out of a doorway, a wicked-looking blade in his hand and a gap-toothed smile on his face. Delia didn't hesitate as years of training kicked in. Before the man could step towards her, her knife slipped from its sheath and found its mark in the man's throat. He looked startled as he realized he was no longer the predator. He fell as blood spurted from his throat. Delia ran over, pulled her knife free and wiped it on his jacket. She placed it back in the sheath and moved past him. She kept running, her body and mind synchronized in their singular goal: escape. The alleys twisted and turned, and Delia used them to her advantage, each bend and break in the path a chance to lose the men behind her.

Delia veered onto a wider street, her pace unrelenting. The shadows of old buildings rose around her, and she used them like a cover. Every step, every breath was calibrated for survival. The mission hung in the balance, but she couldn't think about that now. She had to focus, had to stay a step ahead.

The city loomed large and alive, its pulse frenetic. But Delia had been here before, in different cities with different dangers.

She was at home in the chaos, the gravity feeding her resolve rather than stripping it away.

She ducked into another alley, the sound of pursuit closer than she would have liked. She pulled her silenced pistol from her shoulder holster and shot out a light that hovered over the alley. Darkness surrounded her. A welcome friend. She stepped into a doorway. She heard three sets of footsteps enter the alley, and she waited, her hearing focusing on the footsteps.

When the time was right, she stepped from the doorway, identified her targets and fired. Three bullets left her pistol, and each man fell, a small bloody hole centered in their foreheads. She returned her pistol to her holster and turned. Her eyes searched for a break in the path, a way to disappear and gain precious ground. At the next intersection, the answer appeared as a crowded tram.

Delia didn't hesitate. She darted across the tracks, narrowly avoiding the slow-moving vehicle, and plunged into a pack of tourists on the other side. They carried backpacks and wore bright shirts, an impenetrable wall of leisure that she slipped through with practiced ease.

The crowd moved at an unhurried pace that hid Delia's haste, buying her the time to reassess and regain her lead. She pulled her scarf from her neck, letting her hair fall free as she stripped away any remnants of her previous disguise.

She ran swiftly, moving farther into the city's maze and away from danger. The shadows around her weren't allies; they became points of exposure, places where she could be caught if she wasn't careful. She didn't dare look back, not yet.

Delia wound through the city, each turn deliberate, her trajectory impossible to track. Her pursuers were still out there, but she was pulling away. Her chest heaved, and her thoughts whirled, calculating and recalibrating as she moved.

She doubled back on herself twice, crossing the same square from different directions until she was dizzy from the turns. It was a tactic she'd perfected over the years, and she could feel it working now. The chaos at the club gave her an advantage, and the tangle of Istanbul's streets amplified it. She could hear sirens and saw the flashing lights as several police cars arrived at the club.

After an hour of backtracking, her hotel came into view, and Delia was safe for the moment. She stepped into an alley across from the small hotel, blended into the shadows and waited. She watched the entrance for an hour until she was confident that she had not been followed. She stepped from the shadows, covered her head with her scarf and stepped into the small lobby. Seeing no threat, she raced up the stairs and slipped into her room.

The danger had been too close, and she thought about how they knew she was there. Kemal was the only one who knew where she was headed. She hated to believe that after all these years he would betray her, but she promised herself she would pay him a visit once this mission was over.

She grabbed a quick shower and poured herself a glass of wine from a bottle she had picked up earlier in the evening. She sat and thought about the conversation she had heard in the bar. The consequences of the men's conversation loomed large. Delia had more than she started with, and she was still in the game.

The syndicate had played their hand. They knew she was in Istanbul. But that meant she would have to move faster, dig deeper. Her resolve solidified, unyielding. They would come for her again, but Delia would be ready.

The Analyst's Warning

Delia moved through the shadows of her hotel room, more ghost than flesh as the lamps lit her haunted form. Istanbul's dimming sky framed her solitude. Case files and weaponry spread across the desk, their sharp angles softened by the dusk.

The ring of the secure phone sounded like an accusation, breaking her concentration and affirming her worst fears. Harper's message read like an echo of suspicion: **Official interference, the move toward diplomatic solutions could jeopardize Tommy's life.** Her jaw clenched, a tick of frustration, and her fingers tapped out a restless impatience.

Delia paced the small space, her mind looping through the events at the club. Her careful plans had exploded into chaos, the syndicate's men closing in before she even confirmed the intel. She imagined herself cornered, trapped, her identity blown. Her heart raced at the memory of how close it had been, how it could happen again. She couldn't shake the feeling of eyes on her, even in the privacy of her hotel room. Every shadow seemed like a threat, the night creeping in with its cool fingers, wrapping around her as she fought to keep it all from closing in.

When the phone chimed she snatched it up, her pulse hammering in her throat as she read the encrypted message.

Harper, a friend from long ago, another lifetime. He was a CIA analyst and had been stationed in Istanbul for almost a decade. They had met when she was on assignment for the Organization, a mission to take out a warlord trying to make a bad global situation worse. He had provided her with critical information that helped her accomplish her mission.

He was a strange duck. Average height and geeky. Long hair, always a mess, stubble on his chin and thick glasses. He wore Hawaiian shirts and shorts with flip-flops. He also had an affinity for odd hats. The first time Delia met him, he was wearing a floppy hat with Mickey Mouse ears protruding from the top. He told her once he never had to worry about disguises. He was not your typical government employee. But despite his looks, he was the best intelligence analyst Delia had ever met.

He was her first call as soon as she landed in Istanbul. What Delia liked about him was he never asked questions when she called. He understood her situation with the Organization, and that didn't change things. He considered Delia a friend, and if she needed help, he was there.

The message was to the point. **Government's slow-moving**, the message began. **Trying to negotiate. They are willing to risk alerting kidnappers and put the boy in more danger.** She scanned the rest, her eyes narrowing. Each word confirmed what she'd feared, what she knew from the start. The diplomats would play this by the book, even if it meant Tommy's life. Her fingers gripped the phone, a muscle in her jaw twitching.

A text came through. **So far, they don't know about you. They believe Morrison has reached out to someone but can't confirm who. Be careful.**

Followed by one more. **Locals are looking into 4 murders in the waterfront area.**

Delia set the phone down, Harper's warnings echoing in her mind. She imagined the discussions, the power plays, the callous disregard for anything but protocol. Each word of the message hammered home her isolation, that she was alone in this. Her anger flared, a heat that flushed her skin as she grappled with the problem. She knew that sooner or later, the embassy would figure out she was here, especially if she kept having to drop bodies. The last thing she needed was local interference.

The room seemed to contract, closing in around her. If the government found out she was involved and went public, she would be exposed. No cover. No allies. Her breath quickened. She would not let that happen and risk Tommy's life.

Harper's message was both a curse and a blessing. It confirmed she was still operating in the shadows, for the moment at least. If she moved fast enough, the government wouldn't have time to interfere. Her thoughts snapped back into alignment. She could do this, even without support. She couldn't rely on anyone else.

She let the anger focus her, sharpen her. If she succeeded, if she brought Tommy back, it would give her leverage—enough to hold off the Organization, to reclaim the freedom she thought she'd lost, even though deep inside she knew she could never stop looking over her shoulder.

She dropped into a chair, her eyes falling on the tools and files spread out before her. Harper's message gave her a new direction, but the personal stakes preyed on her mind. The silence closed in, her isolation magnified by the doubts she'd kept at bay. It was necessary for her to compartmentalize, to shove those emotions back into a place where they couldn't reach her.

Delia's fingers tapped an uneasy rhythm on the table. She wanted to believe in him, needed to, but the cost of that trust was more than she was willing to pay. Her life had been built on betrayals. The echoes of the past reverberated through the room, Elena's voice blending with Morrison's desperation.

Elena Petrova had been her friend, her confidant and her lover. They were both recruited by the Organization while still in their teens. They had trained together, shared a life together and killed together, until the mission where Elena had betrayed her, almost getting her killed. The hardest thing Delia had ever done was shooting Elena on that bridge in Baltimore and watching her body sink into the inky depths of the river, only for her to reappear during Delia's last assignment with the Organization. On that mission, Delia had been forced to kill Elena again. This time, she would not be coming back from the grave. Delia shook her head. She wasn't going to live in the past. The boy was all that mattered now, the innocence that hadn't yet been destroyed.

The minutes ticked by, each one pulling her further into her thoughts and further from the fear. Tommy. She could see his face, the trusting eyes that stared out from the photo Morrison gave her. The same vulnerability that had drawn her in and had pushed her to take the mission against her better judgment. The Organization had trained her too well, and Morrison knew which strings to pull. It was time to refocus, to turn this crisis into an opportunity.

She grabbed a map and spread it over the scattered papers. Delia's resolve solidified as she moved the pieces of her plan into place. She thought about Tommy, not just as a boy, but as a kid like her. Alone, scared and counting on someone who would risk it all. Her fingers stopped drumming, her mind re-centering, determination blotting out the doubt and fear.

The world outside moved in its own rhythm, the city alive with its indifference to her struggle. She pushed back against it, shutting out everything but the mission. Her breath slowed, and her grip on the situation tightened. Istanbul glowed in the darkness beyond the window, but in the confines of the room, Delia was still.

Harper's warning wasn't just words. It came with a package: satellite imagery of a compound on the city's edge. Delia's pulse quickened as the file downloaded to her encrypted laptop, the images revealing a puzzle of concrete and steel. Her gaze sharpened, slicing through the dim light, the screen casting her face in cool determination. Each photo mapped the terrain: guard rotations, blind spots, tactical opportunities. A small figure being led from a van into the building, their head covered with a bag, caught her eye. The shape was unmistakable, the vulnerability exposed. She knew it had to be Tommy.

She checked the time stamp on the image. Last night. While she was being chased through the back alleys of the waterfront, Tommy was being moved to a new location. She was unaware of the transfer schedule but needed to move fast before he was moved again.

The tension in Delia's chest unwound as she reviewed the images. They provided a sense of security, something solid to hold on to. A possible location after days of grasping at shadows and avoiding detection. The blue light from the laptop screen soaked the room, a stark contrast to the soft lamplight and her growing certainty. She cycled through the images, eyes narrowing as she noted each detail. Her instincts told her this was it, that Tommy was close. She leaned in, absorbed the pictures and the hope they offered.

One image showed the compound from a distance. A concrete structure surrounded by high walls topped with razor wire, its architecture utilitarian and imposing. Delia's focus sharpened as she traced the perimeter with her gaze. The guards moved in a pattern, predictable and routine. Her breath steadied as she marked their positions, logging the flow of their patrols. The images were sharp, capturing vehicles parked at intervals, hinting at the syndicate's resources and vulnerabilities. As she clicked through each image, the overwhelming complexity of what she was doing transformed into something manageable.

Every angle was accounted for, and the compound appeared in both daylight and infrared. Delia's confidence grew with each frame. The construction was solid, but she spotted weak points where security was lighter than the rest.

Her attention flicked over entryways, escape routes and the subtle signs of a facility not as impenetrable as it seemed. Her mind charged ahead, calculating options, running scenarios. The images brought the target into focus, and she experienced the thrill of anticipation she hadn't allowed herself since taking the mission.

Delia zoomed in on the second story of the building, her breath catching as she saw the shape of a small figure. The silhouette stood near a window. Could it be Tommy, or were there other children in the complex?

Her heart leaped, a rare burst of emotion tightening her throat. Tommy was all she could see. Alone. Scared. Exactly what she'd vowed to prevent. She swallowed hard, fighting to control the rush of feelings. It was him. She was sure of it. And she wouldn't fail him.

The image of Tommy—and she believed it was him—in that window became an anchor, centering her focus and igniting her determination. Delia shifted into tactical mode, her fingers a blur on the keyboard as she scrutinized the remaining images. She identified additional entry points, the paths of least resistance and areas where a distraction could draw attention away from her approach. The more she studied, the clearer the possibilities became.

The surrounding terrain confirmed her suspicions. Located on Istanbul's outskirts, the compound fit what she'd learned from Kemal and the intel she had gathered on the syndicate. A remote enough area for them to operate, yet close enough to the city for them to disappear if threatened. Delia's mind connected the dots, the rigorousness of her training clear in how she evaluated the site. She moved fast; the certainty of Tommy's presence pushed her onward.

The excitement mingled with the critical nature of her situation. Delia glanced back at the laptop. Each image was a promise and a challenge, the stakes enormous but exhilarating. She couldn't waste any time. The government wouldn't be the only ones looking to interfere. If she didn't act now, the syndicate could move him, and she'd be left with nothing but cold trails and regret.

With a last look at Tommy's silhouette, Delia shifted into mission planning. The truth of the boy's plight drove her like a force of nature, consuming her previous doubts. The room pulsed with energy, and she absorbed it all, her focus absolute as she sketched out a rescue plan.

The room transformed into a strategist's sanctum, the detritus of espionage taking shape under Delia's meticulous hands. Images layered like shadows, a collage of intel blanketing the desk and the bed. The demands of an unsupported mission sharpened her focus, each constraint a challenge.

Her equipment gleamed in the soft light: a silenced pistol, lockpicks, night vision goggles and her knives. It was her orchestra of survival, her symphony of risk. She placed Tommy's photo beside the plans.

Morrison had chosen his most recent photo from the American School. His uniform—white shirt, red, white and blue striped tie and blue blazer—showed a young man just coming into his own, his eyes bright and his smile brimming from ear to ear. He was a handsome boy, and she could see his father in his cheerful face.

She stepped over to the window and looked between the crack in the blinds. The city's pulse was relentless outside the window, unaware of the high-stakes planning going on inside.

Delia inventoried her supplies with the meticulousness of a surgeon. The tools were minimal but critical, the bare essentials that could spell the difference between success and failure. Each item became part of a planned arsenal: the dark tactical gear designed for stealth and silence. Her hands arranged the equipment in a seamless flow. The room's soft light played off the metal and plastic, turning them into instruments of purpose.

She sketched the compound layout from memory, the map expanding as her mind connected it to the images. Her notes filled the margins: entry routes, timed rotations and contingency plans. Every movement had a counter, every gap ripe for exploitation.

The absence of backup forced her to consider each angle, each scenario, with a singular intensity. Delia saw it as an advantage. Fewer variables. Fewer people to trust. She thrived under this kind of pressure, where the constraints honed her focus.

Her preparations turned methodical, an efficient rhythm driving her actions. She packed extra ammunition, securing it alongside the silenced pistol. The black fabric of her tactical clothing lay folded, ready for quick deployment.

Delia tested each piece of equipment, and the room filled with the sounds of electronics booting up and snaps locking into place. She memorized the plan, embedding it into her consciousness with an almost obsessive clarity. It wasn't just about getting Tommy out; it was about anticipating every complication and overcoming it.

The night closed in, the edges of Istanbul darkening through the hotel window. The isolation pressed in with the shadows, a silent acknowledgment that she was doing this alone. It was a feeling she knew too well, but this time the risks were greater. No Organization to call in favors. No David to provide a fallback. The thought gnawed at her for a moment, an indication of just how exposed she was.

Delia reviewed the plan once more, her eyes skimming the map with a thoroughness that left nothing to chance. She marked the last guard rotation, the last potential weak spot, with confident strokes. Her mind worked through the timeline again, refining it until it sang with exactness. This was her element, the world of tactics and outcomes, of decisions that left no room for doubt. She embraced the risk, the very real possibility of failure, as an old adversary she would outmaneuver.

Her movements remained fluid and sure, each preparation adding to the certainty that she could pull this off. Delia picked up Tommy's photo, the boy's face innocent against the harsh truth of the operation. She was the one who could do this, and it had to work.

Traffic and distant voices seeped into the room, a counterpoint to the intense focus that enveloped her. Delia inhaled, centering herself as she visualized the operation. The plan was ambitious, but she had left no detail unchecked, no possibility unexamined. With Tommy's life on the line, there was no room for hesitation. She set her jaw, every fiber of her being aligned with the mission.

The night embraced Istanbul as Delia completed her preparations, the time ticking away with increasing urgency. The scene in the hotel room was complete: a strategist's war room, a solo operative's command center.

She sensed the adrenaline build, not from fear, but from the knowledge that everything was in place. Her isolation was not a weakness but a weapon, honed and ready. Delia took a last look at the plans, at Tommy's photo, at the tools of her trade. She would succeed. She had to.

Then, like a note resolving a chord, she was out the door.

Close Encounters

Delia crouched low on the rooftop, the city sprawling beneath, a tangled web. Shadows pooled in the alleyways and across the distant streets, the night stretching its limbs around her in a suffocating embrace. She worked with a hunter's focus, setting up her surveillance gear with methodical accuracy. Each piece of equipment became an extension of her purpose, speaking to her expertise and deliberate intent.

The hum of the city was distilling into the relentless cadence of her pulse. Before her, the compound loomed, a two-story fortress of concrete and silence amidst the surrounding chaos.

Through her camera's cold, indifferent lens, Delia tracked the movements of several armed guards. She froze their images, documenting their routines with the detached clarity of an architect. The figures traversed the compound, predictable arcs that she dissected with an expert eye for detail. Minutes turned liquid, shifting and elongating with each rotation.

In the city, the call of a muezzin echoed through the night, its haunting melody punctuating the stillness and reminding Delia of the stakes. She remained vigilant throughout the night.

Delia tracked the SUV through her lens, its dark presence unsettling as it neared. The diplomatic plates were a sign of influence, breaking the night's routine. Guards shifted, more like servants than soldiers, their deference immediate as the gate swung wide. Her camera caught it all, frames of suspicion and fear.

The man slipped out of the SUV like a shadow, black-clad and dangerous, his blond hair stark under the light. This was what she had come for. Blume walked with deliberate purpose, each step heavy with meaning. Delia focused on him, snapping photos of the meeting between him and the bearded man who stepped out of the building and hugged him like a brother. They spoke for a second, then moved towards the door.

The men pushed open the door and stepped inside. The door closed. Somewhere a tile slipped from a roof, shattering the silence. Delia's breath caught. A guard's flashlight clicked on and scanned the rooftops.

She tightened her grip on the camera, every instinct on high alert. She grabbed her backpack and ducked behind the ridge of the roof and slid down. She landed on a rooftop patio. There was a ladder at the far end of the patio, and she moved towards it, staying low.

The SUV's appearance was a bonus, and it revealed the locations of more guards than she had seen in the satellite images. She also knew where the transfer of documents would take place, and that information was valuable. She heard more guards join the first, and several of them left the compound and headed into the streets and alleys, looking for the source of the noise.

The tension of the night unwound, each second a fracture of control. Delia listened to the guards swarming like a disturbed hive, Blume's entrance the center of their universe. Her heart raced, the thrill of discovery eclipsed by the danger of being caught.

She calmed her breathing to still the chaos that had overtaken her meticulously planned surveillance. But the immediacy was a tidal wave, a force of nature she couldn't escape. Delia weighed her options as the guards converged below.

The scene below her blurred with motion, the flashlight's beam a sharp and constant threat crisscrossing the street. The guards spread out and moved along the street. She ducked behind the low wall, her hand on the ladder, but she held her position until the guards passed by the building she was in.

The guards' movements became more frantic, the shouting more insistent. Delia had seconds, maybe less, before the guards would start checking individual rooftops. She needed a new plan.

Delia's world narrowed to seriousness, every breath a countdown. She grabbed her gear and ran. The guards' shouts rose like a storm. The rooftop stretched before her, a barren wasteland of exposure. She moved with skill and determination.

She spotted a drainpipe running down the wall of the next building. She ran, leaped over the small wall between the buildings and stopped, listening to the guards. The guards were covering the area below but with less immediacy. She hoped that meant they were tired of looking for the source of the noise and would head to the compound. She was not that lucky. The guards sounded like they were standing under the ladder she had just left.

Delia raced across the rooftop and, grabbing the drainpipe with both hands, swung over the low wall and held her position, making sure no one was below her. She slid down the pipe and bolted for the nearest alley, moving away from the guards who were watching one of their associates climb the ladder to the roof she had left moments before.

The city was a traitor and an ally, dead ends and escape routes in every direction. She could hear footsteps moving all around her. She slipped down a narrow alley, her breath ragged and quick. She knew Istanbul well, and she knew the streets and alleys would help her escape.

Adrenaline carried her, the night blurring around her as she raced from alley to narrow street to alley. She had to keep moving, driven by instinct and the knowledge of what capture would mean. The alleys twisted and turned, each corner a potential salvation or trap. She didn't slow to consider which, relying on the instincts and training that had kept her alive this long.

The guards' shouts came from several directions, and she laughed to herself. Had they been quiet in their quest, they would have stood a better chance of capturing whoever they were chasing. Delia navigated by instinct, her body attuned to the rhythm of pursuit. The alleys were a maze, familiar yet foreign in the dark. She ducked low, her silhouette disappearing and reappearing in the patchwork of light and shadow.

Her thoughts raced with each footfall, recalibrating with the terrain's shifts. The night air was cool, but she could feel the heat of exertion, of adrenaline pumping through her system. She forced herself not to think beyond the next turn, the next breath, the immediacy of escape.

A narrow street appeared ahead, its emptiness a risk but also a promise. Delia darted towards it, her heart hammering a rapid beat. The guards were closer now, their pursuit pulling them in tight formation behind her. The alleys funneled their sounds, amplifying them until they pressed against her like a second skin.

She wondered if the guards had picked up on her, a misstep or sound that she hadn't realized she had made. It sounded like they were moving in her direction. Then a thought hit her. What if they were using a drone? She hated to admit that she hadn't even considered the possibility. She was mad at herself. The time spent lying on the beach had diminished her skills. She would rectify that when she got back to her enclave, but for now she had to move.

She pushed herself harder, the world a blur of motion and sound. Her breath came in sharp bursts, and she fought to keep it steady, to maintain control even as the chaos threatened to overtake her.

Delia's instincts pulled her down a side path, narrower than the others. Her shoulders brushed the walls as the city closed in around her. It was both prison and freedom, a duality that thrilled and terrified in equal measure.

A guard appeared, his presence a jolt of danger. He was as surprised as she was, but Delia reacted on pure reflex, grabbing a glass bottle from the ground and hurling it with all her strength. It shattered. The sound was a perfect distraction. She didn't wait to see his reaction. Her body was already in motion, squeezing into a passage wide enough to accommodate her.

The risk paid off, the noise enough to stall the guards' advance. Delia used the seconds it bought her, her pace relentless as she emerged from the narrow streets. The night opened, and she ran with renewed speed, Istanbul sprawling around her in all directions.

She wound through the streets, her path erratic and difficult to follow. Her mind assessed every move, each twist and turn a strategic decision. The adrenaline fueled her, but she knew it wouldn't last. She had to lose them for good.

A glowing sign promised refuge, and Delia made for it, the chance too tempting to resist. She slipped through the doors of a late-night teahouse, its interior dimly lit and crowded. She wove through the patrons, her conviction masked by the calm inside.

The teahouse was a pocket of serenity, its quiet a stark difference from the frenzy outside. Delia blended into the scene, adjusting her posture and pace to match the other patrons. She stayed low, her back hunched as if she were deep in conversation.

She stepped up to the counter and ordered tea and a biscuit. She took them to a table near the rear and took a seat. She pulled her pistol from her holster and set it on the seat, pushing it close to her leg to hide it from view. She sipped her tea and watched as several guards ran past the large front window, never slowing as they continued their pursuit.

She remained in her seat and sipped her tea, her escape complete. After forty minutes, she slid from her seat, walked through the teahouse and entered the street. The street looked like a festival, with tourists and locals partaking in the restaurants, bars and shops that lined it. She slowed her pace, slipping through the city with practiced ease. She was tired and spent, but the exhilaration of survival pulsed through her veins.

When she stopped, Delia was breathless but safe. She leaned against a wall, letting herself feel the full weight of the night's events. The chase had been close—too close. But she had the photos. She had what she came for.

She walked to her hotel and slipped into her room, leaving the lights off. She grabbed the bottle of wine off the counter, poured herself a drink and sat at the small table. She pulled the camera out of her backpack. She flipped through the digital images, her eyes lingering on the ones that mattered most. Blume, the man he met and the briefcase. Delia's heart rate slowed as she reviewed them, the significance of what she'd captured sinking in.

The odds were long, but they always had been. Delia had what was necessary to continue. The risk was real. The mission was more dangerous than ever, but she was still in the game.

A Mole in the Ranks

The cafe was alive, a din of conversation blending with the hiss of steaming cups. Delia entered with the ease of a shadow, her eyes finding Harper at a corner booth. He looked like he hadn't slept in days, a tech analyst with a nervous smile and jittery hands. He wore a ball cap with a shark head on top, its mouth open, exposing its fabric teeth. Delia approached, her presence both calming and commanding. Harper fidgeted, pulling out a tablet concealed beneath a newspaper.

"It's worse than we thought," he murmured, words tumbling over one another. "We have a mole in the embassy. Someone high up." Delia's eyes hardened.

Harper's relief was palpable when she sat down. "This goes to the top," he said, fingers flying over the tablet, pulling up files with rapid efficiency. "I can't believe we're risking meeting like this." He pushed the device towards her, anxiety threading through his voice.

Delia remained impassive, her eyes scanning the screen with cold elegance. "You're certain?" she asked, her skepticism veiled.

Harper nodded, his confidence tinged with fear. He pulled up encrypted message logs, pointing out the patterns with a finger that trembled.

"It's all here," he insisted, leaning in as if the act would keep their conversation from prying ears. "Look at the time stamps. The communication patterns are unmistakable."

Delia followed him with her gaze, her expression unreadable. "A leak this big, and you think it's the ambassador?" Her disbelief was clear, but so was the way she absorbed every detail.

Harper showed her a list of names of high-ranking officials that read like a who's who of betrayal.

Harper met her gaze, eyes wide with the seriousness of his claim. "Someone with top-level clearance is leaking operational details."

He swiped through more files, laying them out like a damning sequence of cards. Each swipe seemed to fray his nerves a little more.

Delia absorbed the information, her expression shifting from skepticism to contemplation to a tight-lipped resolve. The implications pressed on her, heavy and dangerous. She let her eyes linger on the ambassador's name.

Her focus wavered as she glanced past Harper's shoulder. Two men seated at separate tables seemed too interested in their meeting. She stilled, the shift in her posture imperceptible to anyone but Harper, who could feel her tension like an electric current.

"What's wrong?" he asked, eyes darting, a touch of panic creeping in.

Delia looked at him, her gaze sharp and direct. "Stop fidgeting. We're being watched," she whispered. The news turned Harper's face pale, his bravado crumbling.

"What do we do?" he whispered, the fear in his voice unmistakable.

Delia leaned back, appearing relaxed despite the danger that closed in. "When I stand up, wait thirty seconds, then take the back exit," she instructed, her voice calm but urgent.

Harper swallowed, his earlier resolve turning to apprehension. "Are you sure?" he asked, his confidence as fragile as his youth.

Delia nodded, already planning her next move. "Don't look back. Just get to the embassy as fast as you can," she advised.

The words hung between them, a command and a promise. She rose, leaving payment on the table as if concluding nothing more than a casual meeting. Harper watched her go, a measure of doubt and determination in his eyes.

Delia left the cafe with practiced ease, her pace calm and confident. The street was a rush of sound and motion, a sea of bodies she navigated like an unseen current. She sensed the watchers' eyes on her, their gaze hot on her back.

One man stood and followed. The other stayed behind, speaking into a concealed device. Delia quickened her pace down a side street, a narrow passage that offered cover and confusion. The first tail emerged, his eyes locking onto her. She led him deeper, Istanbul a living maze that swallowed them whole.

Her stride lengthened, the city unfolding in vibrant chaos around her. Vendors hawked spices and textiles, the colors and sounds a flurry of distraction. Delia wove through the stalls with specificity, her path deliberate and misleading. The tail kept his distance but didn't hide his actions.

She let the crowds swallow her, moving fluidly through the tangle of marketgoers. The noise was overwhelming, a symphony of bargaining and movement. Delia used it to her advantage, the cover of confusion buying her time. She darted down a new path, her pursuer catching sight of her just as she turned the corner.

The chase wound into a courtyard, tourists milling about with cameras and guidebooks. Delia lost herself among them, the swarm of visitors a perfect camouflage. The man hesitated, his eyes scanning the throng, frustration carving lines into his face. But he didn't lose her.

She moved strategically, the city her ally and her enemy. Each step pulled him further in, each twist in her route a quantified risk. Her breathing remained consistent; Delia could hear the blood in her veins, the adrenaline that sharpened her senses. She was in control, but just barely.

The passage narrowed as they moved deeper, her path weaving through old buildings and hanging laundry. She glanced back, her eyes catching the struggle in his, the relentless drive that pushed him. Delia created more distance, the streets becoming familiar as she doubled back towards her starting point.

She stopped at the entrance to the alley, the stone floor wet from the passing storm. Cigarette smoke hung in the air like a haze. Delia pressed her back to the crumbling brick, instincts counting the half seconds of her tail's approach.

He had the arrogance of a man sure of his quarry, the kind who expected a cornered animal rather than an apex predator. When his frame darkened the entrance, she pivoted on her heel, her movement a violent punctuation against the alley's silence.

The man registered surprise before Delia closed the distance, her body a whipcord blur. He lunged, thinking brute force would suffice, but she sidestepped with practiced indifference and let him overextend. Her elbow crashed into his temple. His forward momentum sent him sprawling into the opposite wall. There was a sickening wet smack as his head rebounded off the plaster, but he was trained, and he didn't go down. Instead, he reached beneath his jacket, a pistol clearing the holster.

Delia's heel struck his knee before he could steady his aim. The kneecap moved in a direction it was never intended to move in with an unnatural pop, and the man screamed, the sound guttural and animal. He collapsed on all fours, the pistol clattering in a useless spiral towards the alley's trash-stained gutter. Without slowing, Delia grabbed his wrist, twisted and wrenched the arm behind his back, dragging him up by the collar of his cheap gray suit.

He twisted, wild and stunned, face slick with sweat and disbelief. "Don't!" he started, but Delia drove her knee into the bridge of his nose.

Cartilage shattered; blood exploded from both nostrils, painting his lips and chin in bright red. He made a noise, high and pathetic, and sagged. Delia let him hit the ground hard, then planted a boot squarely on his throat, pinning him flat beneath her.

The man flailed, clawing at her ankle, making wet, gurgling pleas. Delia leaned in, her weight calibrated for pressure but not quite death. His eyes, sharp and predatory a moment before, now bulged with panic, darting from her face to the Beretta just out of reach.

"Who sent you?" she demanded.

The man gasped, her foot unyielding as she applied pressure to his throat. His eyes bulged with anger and fear. Delia's heart raced, but her hold was steady, her interrogation quick and relentless.

"Talk," she ordered, giving him just enough air to speak. He sputtered, but she read the defiance in his expression. He was going to be hard to break.

Her own vulnerability loomed large, the exposure gnawing at her calm. She had seconds before the other man closed on Harper. She reached into his pocket and pulled out his ID. State Department. Fuck, the secret was out. The embassy knew she was here. Her timeline had just shrunk.

She pulled the pistol from his shoulder holster, pulled out the magazine and ejected the round in the chamber. She smacked him in the head with the gun, and his lights went out. She tossed the gun and magazine onto the lower roof next to her, put his phone in her back pocket and dashed in the direction she knew Harper would take to the embassy. She knew where she would intercept the second agent.

Her feet were moving before she could think, carrying her deeper into the web of streets. She spotted Harper looking like a scared rabbit as he double-timed down the street, the embassy gate just a few blocks away. His head never stopped moving as he scanned the surrounding area. He passed a narrow alley as he moved. Delia waited.

She spotted the second watcher and moved between traffic. Her timing needed to be perfect. The watcher's foot passed one side of the alley, and Delia hit him with a massive body block. The watcher flew sideways and crashed into the alley, his arms flailing as he tried to stop himself. He hit the ground hard and was stunned.

As he reached down to push himself up, Delia slammed her foot onto his wrist. Bones cracked, and he opened his mouth to yell. The rapid right landed before his scream could arrive, and his head whipped back, and he lay still.

Delia looked out of the alley to make sure no one was watching. She pocketed the second cell phone and stepped onto the street. She moved towards the embassy, the adrenaline giving her speed and focus. Her breath was sharp and rhythmic, in sync with the pounding of her heart. Her knowledge of the city had played to her advantage once again.

Delia watched Harper present his ID to the marine guard at the gate, and he entered the complex. He was off the street, but if the information he had uncovered was true, then he had just walked into the lion's den, and Delia was unable to help him.

Delia veered across the street and walked past the embassy on the opposite side of the street. She headed for her hotel. It was time to absorb the information Harper had laid on her. She had been concerned when Morrison said the embassy was being no help in locating his son. Now she wondered if Tommy's abduction wasn't part of a much grander plan, and who was pulling the strings.

Blume had arrived at the compound the night before in an SUV with diplomatic plates, but she never got a clear enough shot to see which government the plates belonged to.

Delia slowed, the impact of recent events settling over her like a shroud. The adrenaline ebbed, replaced by the satisfaction of survival. She was spent but alive, every step drawing her further from immediate danger.

Like the night before, Delia had won this round, a triumph of instinct and skill, but she wondered when that skill and instinct would fail her. Harper would be safe for now, and so would she. Delia had more questions than she had earlier, and she was not comfortable in that position. She hated not knowing.

Morrison's Dilemma

Delia navigated through the Grand Bazaar, her pace more deliberate than her heartbeat. Vendors pushed their goods, and the din swelled, every shout and gesture magnifying her solitude. When she stopped at the spice seller's stall, her thoughts turned inward, charting strategy and risk. She positioned herself in its shadows, checking the pin on her phone that she had sent earlier, knowing Morrison would find her.

He arrived, a picture of unraveling desperation, his presence raw against the market's chaos. She directed him to a nearby coffee shop, its worn awning a welcome sight in the crowded maze. Here, conviction brewed stronger than the coffee.

Morrison slumped into a chair, his face drawn and weary. Dark circles pooled beneath his eyes, and his suit was as rumpled as his composure. He looked like he hadn't slept or changed since they last spoke.

Delia's eyes swept over him, taking in the signs of his deterioration with a detachment she had to maintain. Her fingers tapped the table, like the ticking clock that loomed over them.

"You look like hell," she said, her voice soft and measured. It was both an observation and an invitation for him to unburden himself.

"Feel like it too," Morrison admitted, his voice a fragile thread. He leaned into the table, hands shaking as they cradled a steaming cup. "They've made contact."

Delia's gaze sharpened, her focus narrowing to his words. "And?"

He took a sip, the hot liquid burning away some of his hesitation. "They want the plans. The stealth fighters. In exchange for Tommy."

A muscle tightened in Delia's jaw, a sign that his words had hit home. "That was expected," she said, hiding the dread that moved through her. "They know you have access, and now they know you're considering it."

Morrison's eyes flickered with guilt and resolve. He reached into his pocket, pulling out his phone with fingers that trembled despite his efforts to steady them. "They sent me proof of life," he said, showing her the screen.

The image was stark against the digital display. Tommy, small and vulnerable, holding a newspaper with today's date. From the picture, Delia could see that Tommy was unhurt, but his eyes showed the fear he was facing. Her chest constricted, and she pushed herself to stay composed, to analyze the details as a professional would.

"They've given me forty-eight hours," Morrison continued, the words heavy with desperation. His voice cracked as he spoke, the façade of strength crumbling. "I don't know what to do."

Delia looked at the photo, seeing more than just the pixels. She saw history repeating itself, a cycle she thought she had escaped. "So, you're considering the trade," she said, the statement blunt and accusatory.

He nodded. "I'm running out of options."

Her eyes stayed on the picture, a battlefield of emotion and duty. The silence stretched, filling the space between them like a chasm. She knew what she should say, how to distance herself, but the image burned too brightly.

"What would you do?" Morrison's plea cut through the noise, through the wall she had built around herself. "He looks so scared."

Delia's resolve faltered, the line between the mission and her empathy blurring. She let herself imagine the fear and isolation Tommy was feeling, a reflection of her own past. The familiarity of it stung, pushing her closer to a truth she didn't want to acknowledge.

The clatter seeped into their conversation, and she could feel Morrison's desperation pulling her in. It was important for her to remain detached, and she needed Morrison composed. She turned over the phone, so the picture faced the table.

"I know what it's like," she admitted, the words as raw as she felt. "To be alone and scared, to feel like there's no way out." She took a breath, her composure fraying at the edges. "But you can't do this, Morrison. You can't give them what they want. There's more at play than you realize."

He gazed at her, a storm of fear and uncertainty in his eyes. "What are you talking about? I don't see another choice."

"There are always choices," she said, though she doubted it even as the words left her mouth. The photo lingered between them, a reminder of the stakes.

Morrison leaned back, his exhaustion more apparent with each passing second. "I can't lose him, Delia. I just can't."

His vulnerability tore at her, unraveling the professional distance she fought to maintain. The pull of his fear was real. She knew the same fear, not for herself but for Tommy. It was all she could do to stay grounded, to hold on to the semblance of control.

The conversation played out like a rehearsal of old wounds, each line delivered with nuance and pain. Delia knew this script too well, but that knowledge didn't make it easier. Her instincts told her to push away, to protect herself from the burden of his despair. But she didn't. She let it seep in, let it become part of her.

The market's chaos faded, leaving the two of them and the impossible choice that lay ahead. Delia's breath was tight, her resolve splintering under the pressure.

"You don't know what it's like to lose everything," Morrison said, his voice breaking again.

But she did. That was the problem. She knew all too well.

The admission lodged in her throat, unspoken but there. She pushed the feeling down deep inside herself and looked into his eyes.

Delia's expression softened. "I told you I would get Tommy back, and I will, but don't do something you'll regret. What good will it do Tommy if you get him back and end up spending the rest of your life in prison for treason? There are things at play here that you are unaware of. This may not be the doings of a rogue syndicate. I can't give you more, but I will figure it out before the deadline."

His silence was an answer, more eloquent than any word. Delia could see the fight leave him, the resignation that had held him captive beginning to loosen its grip.

They sat like that, two conspirators in a battle they couldn't yet define. The sounds of vendors swelled around them, a chorus of drive and consequences. Delia sensed it all—the danger, the connection, the tangled web of her past and present. And she knew that no matter the cost, she would not walk away.

The world beyond the tea shop collapsed, shrinking to the importance of their conversation. Delia leaned in, her words as sharp as her focus.

"This isn't just about Tommy," she pressed, reading Morrison's resistance in his clenched jaw and restless eyes. Her composure was a wall against his rising panic. "It's more than a ransom," she said. "These plans could devastate."

Morrison erupted, his anger breaking through his despair. "I don't care!"

His voice cut through the shop's murmurs, drawing stares from patrons whose curiosity flared, then fizzled. Delia held her ground, his defensiveness fueling her own resolve.

"You're asking me to sacrifice my son for some political agenda," Morrison accused, the bitterness in his voice thick.

"I'm not asking you to do any such thing. I'm asking you to see the bigger picture," Delia countered, her tone cool and insistent. "If those plans get into the wrong hands, it won't just be Tommy at risk. They'll sell to anyone willing to pay—terrorists, hostile governments."

He looked away, hands gripping his knees. "I don't want to hear this," he muttered, but she pressed on.

"They know you have access, Morrison. This was never random." Her voice softened, her own struggle bleeding through. "Tommy was the target all along."

The accusation landed hard, and Delia saw the impact in the slump of his shoulders, the way his gaze flickered with anger and helplessness.

"You think I don't know that?" His voice rose again, tinged with the desperation of a man cornered by more than the kidnappers. "But right now I don't care about national security. I care about my son."

The market's noise seeped into the tea shop, amplifying the tension that hung between them. Morrison's outburst attracted the attention of the other patrons, curious eyes turning their way. Delia noted each look, each potential threat.

"You can't let panic decide," she remarked, her control like a tightrope. "There are other options."

Morrison's frustration was palpable, his body coiled with anxiety. "Easy for you to say," he retorted. "You're not the one who's going to lose him."

The words struck Delia with unexpected force, peeling back the layer of detachment she clung to. The past threatened to unmoor her, to pull her into a current she couldn't swim against.

But she couldn't let him see that. Not yet. Her hesitation cracked her composure, and she fought to restore it before the gap widened.

"If you've already decided to throw away your life and your son's life, then what the fuck am I doing here?" she said, each syllable measured. She hoped her directness would pull him out of his funk. "You asked for my help, because I'm the best at what I do. Let me do my job. I will get Tommy back, and I will make sure that those responsible will pay for what they have put you and the young man through." Her eyes tracked a man in dark clothing moving towards them, a shark tearing through the crowd.

She recognized him from the intelligence files: Blume's operative, dangerous and close. "Don't look, but we're being watched," she said. "Let's browse some stalls."

Morrison followed her eyes, a panicked glance that Delia intercepted with a steady hand. "Stay calm," she urged.

They finished their coffee, stood and left the shop. Delia directed him towards the densest part of the bazaar.

The operative's presence loomed large as they moved, his pursuit both cunning and direct. Delia guided Morrison through the labyrinth, each step deliberate. Her mind looked at all the variables, plotting their path to safety.

The noise enveloped them, a living wall of sound and color. Delia maintained her calm exterior, but she could feel Morrison's fear like a pulse beneath her fingertips.

"This way," she instructed, steering him deeper into the sea of stalls. Her breath was steady, her focus unyielding. But beneath it all, a flicker of her own fear stirred.

Delia's hand tightened on Morrison's arm as they neared a row of fabric vendors, their goods spilling in vivid patterns across makeshift tables. She saw panic rising in him again, his eyes darting to meet hers with unspoken questions.

"What now?" he asked, his voice a taut wire of anxiety.

She kept her tone even, though the urgency pressed hard against her calm. "Just keep moving," she said. "They can't get to us in this crowd."

The operative stayed on their trail, his progress slower through the throng but no less determined. Delia's instincts fired with every step. The awareness of their pursuer heightened her focus.

She angled their path towards the narrow alleys that branched like tributaries off the bazaar's main avenue. Morrison hesitated, his fear threatening to derail them both.

"I don't know how much longer I can do this," he confessed, desperation edging his words.

"You can," she insisted, her own resolve lending weight to the assurance. "We're almost there."

She guided him down a tight corridor lined with baskets of spices, their scent overpowering as the walls closed in. Delia scanned the way ahead, searching for any sign of additional surveillance. The shadows played tricks with her vision, every shape a potential threat.

"Delia." Morrison's uncertainty cut through the din.

"We're fine," she said, though she couldn't be sure. Her mind estimated the odds, weighing their chances against the unknown.

The market's chaos reached a fever pitch as they pressed on, every stall a refuge and a risk. Delia's breath slowed as she prepared herself for what came next, her heart a measured counterpoint to the madness around them.

She noticed Morrison's resolve waver, saw it in the way he slowed, his will tested by fear for his son. It mirrored her own internal struggle, the push and pull of duty and emotion.

She stopped at a stall full of handcrafted wooden toys. "Stand here, and no matter what happens, don't move. I'll be back," she urged.

Morrison stopped and turned to look at her, but like a shadow in the night, she was gone. He stood as she requested. Something told him that with Delia watching out for him, he'd be okay, so he slowed his breathing and moved between the rows of toys, looking for something Tommy might like.

Delia didn't look back, didn't dare acknowledge the danger that moved closer with every step. She trusted the density of the crowd to shield her, the market's relentless energy both ally and enemy.

She reached a junction where three streets converged, and she seized the opportunity to change direction. She spotted her prey at a flower booth. His eyes were fixed on Morrison as he faked interest in the flowers.

Delia reached behind her back and pulled out one of her knives. She pulled the scarf over her head and moved towards the man, who was looking around, instead of being fixated on Morrison. He must have realized Delia was not with him.

He stepped from the flower booth and towards Morrison. Something bumped into him from behind. He stumbled, feeling a burning sensation in his back, and reached behind himself. His hand came away bloody. He spun, trying to find his assailant, but the crowd closed around him. He took two steps and his legs gave out. He collapsed, and the crowd separated.

People gazed at the man on the ground and then noticed the pool of blood forming beneath him. The woman who owned the flower stall stepped over to him and screamed. The crowd moved back, and hundreds of cell phones captured his image as his life left him.

Whistles sounded from every direction, echoing through the streets and alleys of the bazaar. The chaos was instant. Uniformed police surged towards the epicenter of the commotion, the man in the street, face down in a growing pool of his own blood.

Vendors and tourists scattered, many with their cell phones out, taking video of the events, others shoving by, looking to distance themselves from the scene. The Ottoman architecture amplified the cries and the shrill sound of whistles, bouncing them off stone and canvas until they melded with the city's ancient pulse.

Morrison hesitated at the toy stall's edge, his knuckles locked white around a carved wooden dolphin, a gift for Tommy that would never leave the shelf. He stood, transfixed, watching the crowd swarm, watching the police struggle to break through as cell phones documented every gory angle.

Then a hand closed around his elbow. Firm, urgent, no trace of tenderness.

"Time to go," Delia whispered, pulling him back from the encroaching wave of humanity.

She pushed him in a zigzag motion, cutting past two old men bellowing at each other over a backgammon board and a family haggling for prayer beads. Morrison stumbled, his feet unable to keep pace with her strategic movements.

He tugged his arm free just as they ducked past a stall draped in cheap silk scarves. "What did you do?" he demanded, his breath ragged. "Was that . . . was that him?"

Delia paused just long enough to flash the hint of a smile. "I'm tired of being tracked by every shithead contract killer in Istanbul. I sent Blume a message: We're not prey. We're predators now." She sounded almost giddy, as if the act of violence had peeled off some invisible shackle.

"We're going to be on every security camera in the district!" Morrison spat, fear in his voice.

She didn't wait. "We already were. But now they'll be too busy with the blood to notice us slipping out the back." She snatched a paisley scarf off a rack, tossed a crumpled bill to the vendor and wound it around her own head, then grabbed another for Morrison, knotting it tight beneath his chin. "You want to survive? Look local, not diplomatic."

Red-and-blue strobes painted the arcade ahead as a battered ambulance, horn blaring, shouldered its way through the throng. The body at the flower stall had become a grotesque tourist attraction, the crowd behind them thickening into a mass of raised arms and phones. Delia used the chaos like a smoke screen. She ducked Morrison into an alley just wide enough for two abreast.

"Keep your head down," she muttered, glancing up at a security camera with a shattered lens. She checked over her shoulder, seeing three men in Blume's colors—a black leather jacket and dark jeans, the Berlin street thug uniform—pushing through the maze about forty meters behind. They peeled off, one towards the left to cut them off at the next intersection.

Delia's mind ran quick math on the pursuit: they'd have maybe ninety seconds before the first man entered the alley.

Morrison tripped over a piece of broken concrete, catching himself just in time. "Where are we?"

"Trust me," she said, guiding him through a staff-only door marked in Turkish with a faded authorized personnel only sign. Inside, the air smelled of saffron and other spices. Delia locked the door, slid a steel shelving unit across it and motioned for silence.

The storeroom was lit by a single yellow bulb. Boxes teetered in precarious stacks; sacks of spices lined the shelves. Delia flattened herself against the cold masonry, listening for pursuit. Morrison panted beside her, sweat dotting his brow, the scarf making him look less like a father and more like a fugitive.

"Stay," she whispered, and vanished farther into the building.

Morrison tried to slow his breathing, his heartbeat so loud he feared it would give them away. He pressed his back against the wall, feeling the vibrations of heavy footsteps pounding down the corridor outside. There were voices, European, urgent, muffled.

Morrison squeezed his eyes shut as a strange calm washed over him. What would Tommy think if he saw his father like this? Hiding, desperate, trusting a woman he'd met less than forty-eight hours ago. But as he remembered Tommy's small hand in his own, Morrison knew he needed to see this through.

A clatter echoed from deeper in the storeroom. Morrison tensed, ready to bolt, but then saw Delia signal to him from the dark. She'd found a back exit behind stacks of T-shirts and jeans.

"This way," she mouthed. "Quick."

He followed, trusting her implicitly now, moving on instinct. They exited through the back door of the clothing merchant's shop, where a teenager smoked and watched CNN on his phone. Delia pressed a generous tip into his palm and mimed silence. He pocketed the money, grinned and went back to the screen.

They emerged onto a side street, the ruckus of the bazaar now a distant hum. It took nearly a minute for Morrison's legs to catch up with his brain. He yanked the scarf loose, gasping at the sudden rush of cool air.

Delia scanned the horizon. The heights of Istanbul sprawled in their impossible mosaic: minarets, neon, ancient stone, all stitched together by noise and movement.

"We head uphill, towards Taksim," she said, her voice returning to its professional register. "We'll be ghosts before dusk. Blume will turn the old city upside down, but we'll be in his blind spot."

Morrison nodded, not trusting himself to speak.

They walked, sticking to the winding, narrow lanes that tourists avoided. Delia set a hard pace, her stride betraying the faintest limp. Morrison couldn't help but study her as they moved. The way she scanned every window above and every shadowed doorway. The way she flattened herself against the wall at the sound of a siren, and the way her hand never strayed far from the inside of her coat, where a glint of steel peeked from her hip.

After ten minutes, they ducked into the back room of a tiny bodega. Delia produced a burner phone from her purse and entered a coded sequence from muscle memory. She spoke low into the receiver, her Turkish flawless and brisk. Morrison understood none of it but recognized the universal sound of a person calling in a favor.

She hung up and leaned against a crate of oranges. "We have fifteen minutes, maximum, before the entire neighborhood reboots. Blume doesn't accept failure. He'll escalate."

"So, what now?" Morrison said, his voice hoarse.

She wiped a smudge of blood from her fingers with a paper napkin and met his eyes. "You said you want your son back? The only way is to bargain from strength. They think you're desperate. We showed them we're not."

"They'll kill him," Morrison said, his composure slipping.

Delia shook her head. "They're professionals. Professionals don't get paid for dead hostages." She gestured for him to sit, then lowered herself beside him on the battered metal bench.

They sat in silence, the noise of the city leaking in through a cracked window. Delia seemed to relax for the first time since the cafe, her shoulders dropping as she leaned back. Morrison watched her, wondering what it cost to be this unbreakable, and whether the price was always worth it.

A text buzzed on Delia's phone: a single word. She read it and stood. "Our ride is on the next street." She rummaged in a crate, found two baseball caps and handed one to Morrison. "Put this on. Follow my lead." She handed the owner of the shop cash.

He did as she said. Together, they left the shop, stepping out into the golden haze of late afternoon, two strangers with nothing in common but the need to survive.

The clamor of the bazaar was soon behind them, silence engulfing Delia and Morrison as they moved farther from the scene she had created. Delia held Morrison's arm as they walked.

"Don't look back," she whispered.

They ducked into an alleyway lined with copper artisans, the clang of metal on metal shielding their breathless exchange.

"I need twenty-four hours," Delia pressed. "Don't contact the kidnappers." Morrison hesitated, fear etched into every line of his face.

"Every hour puts Tommy in more danger," he said, the words ragged with emotion. "I can't wait."

Delia leaned in, her voice a counterpoint to the pounding of the artisans' hammers. "You can," she insisted. "This isn't just about Tommy. Rushing in will get you both killed."

The crowd in the alley thinned as they neared the next street, the market's noise a dull roar behind them. Delia scanned the street, looking for anything out of place.

Morrison saw her attention shift, his anxiety flaring. "What now?" he asked, his composure as fragile as his trust.

"Just keep moving," Delia urged, pulling him through the last of the artisans' stalls and onto the sidewalk.

The metal clangs masked their footsteps, a staccato rhythm that drove them forward. She didn't wait for him to protest.

They slipped into a small carpet shop, the door jarring against its hinges as they rushed inside. The shopkeeper looked up, surprise flickering across his face before Delia guided Morrison through the stacks of rugs and out the back. The urgency tightened, every second stretching under the stress of their escape.

The rear exit spilled into a quieter section of the market, the paths winding through stalls with leather goods and tourist trinkets. Delia pushed them forward, her pace relentless, her mind working faster than her feet.

"This is crazy," Morrison said, his breath labored. "I don't know how much more of this I can take."

She met his eyes, her determination stark against his desperation. "Yes, you can take whatever you have to take to get Tommy back. We're almost there."

Even though they were far from the bazaar, she continued to lead Morrison through the maze, every turn a strategic maneuver to keep ahead of any more danger.

"You need to trust me," Delia insisted, the sincerity in her voice moving through the chaos. "Twenty-four hours. That's all I'm asking."

Morrison's steps faltered, doubt eroding his resolve. He stopped, his hesitation a tangible force between them. "And if you're wrong?"

"I'm not," she replied, her certainty unyielding. But beneath it, a glimmer of understanding softened her words. "I know it's hard. I know what you're risking."

The vulnerability in his expression was a mirror, reflecting the struggle she endured to separate the mission from her emotions. It was dangerous, but Delia let him see it, let him see her.

She took a breath, pulling back just enough to regain her balance. "This is the only way to save him," she said, the conviction clear and unwavering.

Morrison hesitated, caught between his fear and her confidence. Delia saw the moment his defenses crumbled, the moment he believed in her. "Okay," he relented, his voice a whisper. "Twenty-four hours."

She nodded. The responsibility of his trust was both a burden and a release. "Go back to your residence," she instructed. "Wait for my call."

"And if I don't hear from you?" His question lingered, a manifestation of the breadth of his doubt and the fragility of his hope.

"You will," Delia promised, the rare warmth in her tone surprising them both. She turned to leave, but Morrison's voice stopped her.

"Why are you doing this?" he asked. "When I asked for your help, I never realized how much danger I was putting you in," he asked, the need to understand as powerful as the need to save his son.

She paused, the question resonating with a truth she couldn't quite ignore. "Because I know what it means to lose someone you love," she said, the admission raw and unguarded.

Morrison's expression softened, the fight easing from his features. Delia sensed the connection between them shift, an alliance born from desperation and something deeper.

A black SUV with blacked-out windows sat idling at the curb. The back door opened, and they slipped inside. The SUV pulled away from the curb and melted into the city. They were shadows among shadows, with only the faintest hope that they might come out the other side with all their pieces intact. The SUV dropped them off opposite the American embassy, and they slid out.

They parted, and Morrison headed for the embassy gate. Delia slipped back towards the chaos of the market with the plan forming in her mind. She moved with practiced refinement. She thrived in uncertainty, each turn a deliberate move in the game she was determined to win.

Her breath steadied as the bazaar's noise rose around her, the thrill eclipsing the risks. The images of the night returned, each one a piece of the puzzle she had to solve: Tommy, small and alone; Blume, calculating and close; the operatives, relentless in their pursuit.

Delia knew the burden of it all, sensed the familiar pull of adrenaline and purpose. Her path twisted through the market, every turn taking her farther from Morrison and closer to the truth.

The urgency drove her, pushed her with a speed that defied the chaos she left behind. She didn't look back, didn't let herself question the choices she'd made.

She embraced the uncertainty and impossible odds, treating them like a challenge. It was where she belonged, where she was most alive.

And this time, Delia would not fail.

The Istanbul Ambush

Delia settled into position, the chill of the concrete seeping through her clothing as she watched the building with unblinking focus. Her rifle lay ready, a precision instrument at her command. The scene unfolded below, each movement tracked by her practiced eyes.

The structure was a fortress, its exterior solid concrete. She noted every window, every door and the erratic pattern of the guards. Her mind replayed Harper's intelligence, the memory crisp and clear as she counted heads and potential escape routes. They must have gotten the message, because there were more guards in the compound than there had been the first time she surveilled it.

She took stock of her own readiness, hands grazing over the backup weapons strapped to her body. She was silent and sure, a manifestation of the years she'd spent becoming someone who didn't hesitate, someone who didn't falter. She scanned the landscape through her scope, the view an amplified portrait of danger.

A black SUV pulled up to the gate, entered the compound and pulled to a stop next to the trucks that had entered a few minutes before. Delia watched closely, hoping to see who was in the SUV. The rear door opened, and a figure emerged. The man was tall and wore a hat and a long trench coat. The man walked across the compound to the building.

Something in Delia's mind clicked. She thought she recognized the movement, the pace the man set. There was something distinctive and familiar about it. She focused the camera on the man as he walked, hoping to get a picture of his face. The man turned as he met Blume outside the door. Delia froze; her heart skipped a beat, and she stared without moving. There was no way. It wasn't possible.

She zoomed in tighter on the man's face. There was no doubt about it. The face belonged to David. Her David. But how was that possible? Her chest tightened, but she shook her head to clear her mind. "What the hell is happening? Why would David be here in Istanbul and attending a meeting with Blume?" The two men entered the building and closed the door.

Time blurred, the night measured by the increased activity in the compound. Delia's eyes remained sharp, capturing the unfolding narrative with clinical detachment. She saw vehicles approach, their engines a distant growl in the growing darkness. The men who emerged moved with practiced exactness, each one a puzzle piece sliding into place. Her fingers tightened on the rifle as she recognized several of them from the briefing files. Blume's private army. Their presence confirmed the stakes.

She watched the figures spread out around the compound, noting the subtle shifts in guard positions, the choreography of a careful operation. The windows of the building glowed, the yellow light pooling in odd shapes around the compound. She cataloged the scene, each detail a line in the story she was about to write. Delia prepared herself, the task pulling her into the night's embrace. "Yeah," she thought. "Blume definitely got my message."

Delia measured her breath, a metronome of focus and control. Awareness needled at her thoughts, the meeting below shifting with an undercurrent she couldn't ignore. The scene evolved, and Delia noted the subtle changes in the shadows. A ripple, almost imperceptible, swept across the compound.

The texture of the night was different now, a familiar darkness infused with the flavor of betrayal. Her instincts sharpened, every sense attuned to the threat she could taste but not yet see. It was a trap, but not for her. A sudden flare, metal, and motion igniting the night. Gunfire splintered the stillness, the staccato bursts striking with deadly accuracy at the syndicate's positions.

Delia rolled, trading her camera for the rifle, the concrete biting into her elbows as she moved. Her eyes never left the scene, tracking the explosive shift in the night's narrative. She looked through the scope, the view painted now with violence and chaos.

Blume's men, the same ones she'd seen assemble with military precision, unleashed a brutal barrage on the syndicate's guards. They were outmatched and unprepared, scrambling under the withering fire that poured down on them. It happened fast, faster even than Delia had expected. The men she had watched spread across the compound fell one by one, their bodies dropping as the shots rang out with merciless efficiency.

Every second was long and drawn, a distorted stretch of time where her mind was in overdrive to keep up with the ferocity of the ambush. Delia watched as the orchestrated choreography unfolded into deadly disorder. The syndicate's men, poorly trained and now surprised, never stood a chance against the onslaught. Each one became a statistic in the unfolding carnage, their collapse a testament to Blume's cunning.

Delia's heart beat like a war drum, each thud resonating with the danger that closed in around her. She'd walked into a trap, and the realization hit her like a bullet. Blume had double-crossed the syndicate, but to what end? And what was David's role?

The air cracked around her, pieces of concrete flaking off the building like torn paper as bullets peppered the walls. Delia stayed low. She wondered if she could use the carnage to get to Tommy.

She saw flashes behind the shades inside the building, and fear welled up in her. David was inside, as was Tommy. Could she reach him? Should she even try? Without knowing what was happening, she would be going in blind. The last thing on her mind was to risk his life. She held steady.

The darkness was alive with danger, each shadow a potential threat. She caught the pattern now, the subtle orchestration she should have seen earlier. Blume had played his hand, each position precise and ruthless. Delia's heart pounded with more than exertion—it was anger, raw and unfiltered. She focused it, turned it to fuel as she scanned the scene.

Her rifle was steady. Each shot would be a hint of defiance. But should she take the risk and expose herself? So far, it didn't appear that anyone knew she was there. She saw figures dart between cover, their movements sharp and rehearsed. She saw muzzle flashes below, a chorus of violence that confirmed the scale of the trap. Her vision narrowed, her senses amplifying each detail, each breath, each movement.

Time fractured, her awareness bending it to her will. Delia lined up a shot, let out half a breath and squeezed the trigger. The noise barely registered above the chaos below, but she watched through the scope as one man's head exploded. Delia sighted in on a second figure, firing away with an AR-style rifle. The man died where he stood. Delia fired again, deliberate shots that held back the encroaching tide. The men moved strategically, every angle covered. She counted their positions, memorizing the map of danger that unfolded around her. This was more than a scare, more than a warning. This was going to be a massacre.

She rolled from cover, a fluid motion that bought her a precious second of advantage. It was imperative that she get to Tommy. She knew there was a small door in the concrete wall at the back of the compound. An escape hatch. If she could get to it, she might have a chance.

The world sharpened, each edge clear and unyielding. She embraced the chaos, welcomed it as an old friend. Delia refused to fall into their trap, refused to be the prey. She fired again, a final volley before shifting to a new position. It was a game of survival, and she knew the rules all too well.

The rooftop stretched before her, a battlefield and a trap. Delia's world narrowed to bullet trails and cold wind. She moved like fury embodied, defiant in the face of the storm. A guard dropped, her shot precise and final.

Something slammed into her arm, and she recoiled. The pain in Delia's arm was sharp and searing, a sensation akin to being branded with a hot iron, leaving her skin feeling as though it had been scorched by a fiery blade. The wound pulsated, sending waves of agony through her body, a vivid reminder of the perilous situation she found herself in. Her flesh burned raw and tender, as if every nerve ending was aflame, amplifying the intensity of her plight. She ignored it, intent on escaping.

The ladder came into view, a promise and a threat. She ran for it, desperate speed in every stride. The guard appeared without warning. Delia fired from the hip, and the bullet pierced his skull.

She was across the rooftop in seconds, the path perilous and exposed. Her breath synced to her pulse, a rhythm of urgency that refused to relent. Her shoulder throbbed, the pain sharp and insistent, but she pushed it down, focused on nothing but survival.

Delia seized the ladder, the metal biting into her palms as she swung her body onto the lower level. The guard's attack was swift, his presence sudden and dangerous. She met his assault with the calm of the practiced, her counterattack efficient and brutal.

Their struggle was a ballet of shadows, a silent symphony of violence that echoed with the breathless intent to survive. She ducked a vicious swing, using his own momentum against him. The man's arm snapped with a sickening crack, the sound a punctuation of pain. Delia silenced him with a precise strike, his body collapsing at her feet. She wiped her knife on his coat and pressed on.

The rooftops were a maze, a labyrinth she navigated with instinct and expertise. She moved like smoke, her silhouette a whisper against the industrial backdrop. The courtyard below seethed with activity, but Delia stayed focused, her path clear and unwavering. She wasn't sure if anyone, other than the two syndicate guards she'd encountered, had seen her. She needed to get to the small door without being seen.

She climbed down the ladder and paused under a window at the back of the house. Two men argued over the clamor, their words ripping through the noise like gunshots. Delia stilled, her senses heightened, every nerve tuned to the unexpected revelation.

"This is what happens when you trust a mole! Someone close to Morrison is going to get us all killed!"

She recognized David's voice. She had never heard him this agitated. David was always a calm port in her stormy life. Someone she knew would calm her down and keep her close. This David was unknown to her. A realization hit her, and she shook away the thought. She would deal with that later.

"Just get the boy and let's go," said a German accent. "We need him, or his father will not cooperate."

The comment reverberated through her, a bullet of truth that left her reeling. She absorbed the impact, her mind processing the dangerous implication. The trap had been set up to extract Tommy from the syndicate. The threat to Tommy was far greater than she had imagined.

The gunfire abated as Delia reached the hatch, which stood open, having been an exit for someone seeking refuge from the fight. She shouldered her rifle and slipped through the door. She was inside a small storage room filled with food. It looked like someone was prepared to hold out for a long time in the event of a siege. She guessed they'd never expected the siege to come from those sent to help protect the package.

Delia left her rifle shouldered and pulled out her silenced pistol. The gunfire had stopped, and a deathly silence took over the building. She opened the door to the room a crack and looked outside. Several bodies were strewn about the hallway. Their deaths had been swift. She moved down the hall, her senses on full alert.

She heard David's voice. "Good. Put a hood over his head and let's go. The cops and the military will be here any minute."

She made out a scuffle, and then the German voice. "Hold still, kid, if you ever want to see your father again. Get him out of here."

She risked a look around the corner and saw David and Blume, surrounded by several soldiers, walk towards the door. Tommy was between them. She pulled back. If she opened fire now, Tommy would die. The decision clawed at her, and she hated having to abandon him, but what choice did she have? She heard sirens and didn't want to get in a firefight with the local police and military.

The door closed, and she stepped around the corner. The bearded man who had met Blume the first time she saw him lay dead next to an overturned table, a bullet hole placed between his eyes.

She stepped over the body and snuck a peek through the filthy window. She observed the same diplomatic plates as the last time, but she couldn't read who they belonged to. She memorized the plate number. As soon as she was safe, she would contact Harper and have him trace the plate.

She watched as the SUV pulled through the main gate and disappeared into the night, followed by the trucks containing Blume's army. Blue lights flashed as the police pulled into the yard. Delia headed to the storeroom.

Delia's escape was fast and final, the night's dark expanse wrapping around her like a secret. The words she heard tonight lit a new fire that fueled her flight. She pushed into the darkness, her pace relentless, her focus sharper than ever.

Delia fled into Istanbul's maze of concrete arteries, but she wasn't alone. She could sense them tracking her. Three of them. She wasn't sure if they were what was left of the syndicate or if they were Blume's men, but she wasn't waiting around to find out. She willed her body to move, the adrenaline a hot rush. Her knowledge of the city served her well. She led them through abandoned buildings and narrow corridors. Debris became weapons in her wake, slowing her pursuers, but not enough.

The alleys twisted ahead, a maze designed for escape. Delia darted down the nearest path, her pace relentless and her breath a sharp rhythm. She was a phantom, her movements rapid and unpredictable. The route she took opened up and closed in, its architecture a double-edged ally.

She heard one pursuer fall back. Either too tired to move on or looking for a shortcut to get ahead of her and set up an ambush. Delia surged ahead. She sensed the nearness of the other two, their drive to catch her as strong as her will to avoid them. She couldn't let them catch her, couldn't let them close the trap.

An abandoned building loomed ahead, its gaping door an invitation and a risk. Delia didn't hesitate. She burst inside, the darkness swallowing her. Her footsteps echoed, a cacophony of urgency and speed. She knew the men would follow. She counted on it.

Her path wound through the structure, a rapid descent that used every floor to her advantage. She hurled debris in her wake, blocking sight lines and creating confusion. A haphazard staircase promised both escape and danger. Delia took it without pausing, her feet lightly touching the steps as she ran downward.

One man lagged, the chase taking its toll. Delia pushed harder, knowing she had a chance to lose them. She exploded out of the building's lower level, her body a blur of motion as she hit the streets. Her heart thundered, but she was not yet free.

The last pursuer was tenacious, a shadow that refused to let her go. Delia saw the distance between them shrink, each step bringing him closer. She fought the urge to look back, to see how close he was.

The alley ended in a small square, deserted and dark. Delia didn't slow her pace, a calculation of speed and need. The space was wide, exposed. She had to make her move. Now.

She wheeled around, her body coiled like a spring. The man barreled into the open, surprise flashing in his eyes. Delia struck with intensity, like she had lived this fight a hundred times. Her body became a weapon, every limb an instrument of ruthless efficiency.

The struggle was short and brutal. The man's face met her elbow, the impact staggering. Delia pressed her advantage, a relentless force that gave him no time to recover. Her fists found their mark, her movements quick and unforgiving.

She finished it with a kick that sent him crashing into an abandoned vendor's stall. Wood splintered and broke, the man slumping unconscious among the debris. Delia stood over him for a heartbeat, her breath ragged and her body taut. She wrapped her arms around his head and with a sharp twist heard a crack, and his final breath left his body. She pushed him out of the way.

The urgency screamed at her, pulling at her. She couldn't stay. Not here. Delia sprinted through the alleys, her speed a reckless blur. The city stretched ahead, an endless tapestry of danger and refuge. She had to keep moving, had to find cover.

A half-built construction site rose from the shadows, its skeletal frame a perfect hiding place. Delia collapsed against a stack of metal beams, her body shaking with exertion and adrenaline. Her breathing slowed, the reality of her escape settling in. She had broken free. The night's revelations weighed on her, the implication of Blume's words a new and urgent threat.

The mole was close to Morrison, closer than she had feared. Delia's mind raced, processing the risk to Tommy. The boy was in more danger than she'd imagined. Her need to uncover the truth became a driving force, an obsession. She stood, every muscle protesting. Delia had a new plan, a new path. She couldn't stop. Not now.

Ghosts from the Past

Delia stumbled into the dilapidated safe house, her eyes tracing the crumbling walls and boarded windows. The room inside was dimly lit, the only light coming from an old lamp in the corner. The furniture was old and worn, revealing a history of use and neglect. Dust coated every surface, giving the room an abandoned feel. Despite its rough appearance, Delia was safe within its walls.

The air in the safe house was musty, as if no one had been there in years. But underneath the mustiness, Delia could detect the subtle scent of disinfectant, perhaps a sign of recent cleaning.

Hamza had come through. Locks clicked behind her, a dissonant chorus of relief. Her breath slowed, echoing the thud of her footsteps and the urgency that brought her here. Pain followed her like a faithful dog, leaving traces of red in her wake. Delia collapsed into the nearest chair. She checked her sleeve and for the first time noticed the blood dripping onto her hand. She pulled off her shirt, the agony sharp and honest against the swell of older wounds: A little girl in a closet. Her parents' screams. Her first memory.

The room was dark, the shadows clinging to worn furniture and chipped paint. Delia stood and secured the windows, pulling down blinds until the world was shut out. Her motion was erratic, a patchwork of desperate efficiency and faltering breath. The air smelled of dust and solitude, enveloping her in a cocoon of harsh quiet. She dropped into a chair, her legs trembling under the strain of exhaustion and injury. Blood bloomed like a flower down her arm.

She peeled away the soaked fabric, her fingers shaking as the pain flared. The wounds were bright against her pale skin, a jagged tear across her upper arm, not deep, not as deep as the ache that she couldn't bandage.

Delia pulled a small med kit out of her backpack. She unpacked the contents, lining up gauze and antiseptic with precision. The sight of the medical supplies brought a shuddering breath to her lips, the simple act of tending to herself echoing her loneliness.

The antiseptic burned, a sting that leaped across her skin and into her past. Her eyes closed against the flood of memory, the vivid images cutting deeper than any knife. Her hands were slick with red, and she pressed harder, hoping to stifle the pain before it grew unbearable.

As Delia struggled with the bandages, her focus drifted in and out like the tide. Each wave brought a new flash, a recent memory surfacing with jagged edges. She was young again, small and frightened, the crash of a door splitting her world in two. Her parents' voices rose in desperation, the words swallowed by violence. "You can't do this." A plea. A warning. Then nothing but the memory of her own shallow breathing and the smoke and blood.

The room was silent but for the rasp of her breath. She clung to the details, grounding herself in the tactile reality of her wound.

She remembered how the room went quiet, how the fear turned cold and hard. Her child's mind refused to accept it, each moment a stretch of eternity that left her numb and alone.

Delia's hands moved over her body, binding the gash that cut into her. The movements were disciplined, but the tremor of memory stole the strength from her fingers. She fought against it, wrestling for control as the images blurred and sharpened, their clarity like a curse.

She forced her mind to the task at hand, each pull of the gauze a tether to the now. Her breath came in harsh, uneven bursts, as though each inhalation had to battle through a lifetime of suffocated emotion. She focused on the feel of the fabric, the way it tightened over her skin, trying to lock away the hurt.

The girl in the closet, curled and silent. She remembered holding her knees, the terrible awareness of a world that wasn't safe. A shadow through the crack of the door, the man's boots tracking blood across the floor. Her heart split with the certainty that she was next. But she wasn't next. The man hadn't found her, and she stayed hidden.

When she emerged from her hiding spot, the terrible truth hit her all at once. Her parents' bodies lay in the hallway on the ground floor, bullet holes making a lasting impression on a young girl. The police and paramedics arrived, but there was little to be done, and she was whisked away to a place she didn't want to be.

Delia cinched the bandage, her breath leveling into something close to calm. The flood of memory receded, leaving a raw and aching emptiness in its wake. Her body was an inventory of wounds, each one speaking of both present and past betrayals.

She sat among the clutter of used gauze and open wrappers, the remnants of her solitude scattered around her. Her breath was steady, each exhale a little less ragged than the last. But the silence was heavy, the onus of history pressing down with relentless force. She closed her eyes, but this time she couldn't push back the thought that had come to her when she heard David's voice in the building. David was one of them. Part of the Organization.

She shuddered at the thought. Soft-spoken, sweet David, the man who knew how to hold her and touch her, and make her world seem safe. The man she had shared her body with and was prepared to share her life with. She had been betrayed, but as she thought about it, it all made sense.

She wondered during her escape from the Organization, after she aborted her last mission, why they never went after David to get to her. They knew he was a part of her life. He would have been easy to get to, and she would have given up everything, including her life, to save him. But it never came to that. They pursued her but left him alone. He had also never questioned her long absences when she told him she was working for clients but was really on a mission. Now it made perfect sense, and she bristled at the thought that the one person she trusted in the whole world had betrayed her.

Tears rolled down her cheeks as she thought about a life wasted. But it wasn't wasted. She loved him with all her heart. The only person since Elena she was willing to give her love to. And now, after his betrayal, they were both gone, and she was once again alone.

She surveyed the sterile, impersonal space, her isolation reflected at her on every bare surface. The walls were too close, the air too thick with what she'd tried so hard to forget.

Delia leaned back, the chair creaking under the tension of her body. Her eyes closed, and she allowed herself a brief, fragile moment of nothingness. No mission, no memories. Just the shallow comfort of breathing. But the nothingness wouldn't last.

Her dreams wouldn't let go as she settled into an uneasy state of sleep. The safe house turned cold, the room a cell built from old ghosts. Blood traced paths over her skin, a map of anguish that history wouldn't let her forget. Each breath was shallow, her sleep fractured by unrelenting memories.

The Organization had found her, so small and scared, a child in a foster home. They recruited her for her mind and her empty heart. Trained her until she broke. Made her strong enough to stay that way. Emotions severed. Conscience silent. They called her first kill a training exercise. She called it the start of everything.

Delia leaned against the wall, the light flickering over her like a lie she couldn't escape. Her reflection stared back from a cracked mirror, fractured like her past. She caught the glint of pain in her eyes, an echo of what she'd learned to hide. Each wound reopened another, the effort to stitch them closed more than physical.

The coldness wrapped around her, an embrace as familiar as it was unwelcome. Her breath mingled with the scent of blood, drawing her back to training facilities that stripped away her youth and innocence. She was small again, smart and detached, the perfect candidate for a life of controlled deception. They'd seen her potential and her vulnerability, a child with nothing left to lose.

She thought about the moment they came for her, the suit's immaculate cut and the way he spoke as though she had a choice. "We can give you a new life," he said. A life of discipline, of precision, of betrayal. They called her gifted, and she let herself believe it. A girl no longer alone, but part of something much larger than she ever wanted.

The Organization took her, molding her through force and cunning. She recalled the foster home and how happy she had been to leave. It was the escape she longed for, yet it led to another prison. Delia saw her younger self, haunted eyes that didn't know they would soon be empty. Her intelligence noted, her coldness prized. She learned to suppress the fear, to become what they needed her to be.

Their training was relentless, and the memories wrapped around her like barbed wire. She reflected on the mock trials, the scripted interrogations. Each exercise honed her mind and created the flawless cover of an attorney.

Her youth was spent in simulated courtrooms, her brilliance as much a weapon as the weapons she learned to kill with. Delia could see it all, the harsh lights and harsher lessons, the mentors who taught her to lie, to manipulate, to thrive in a world without trust.

The psychological conditioning left her raw and exposed, a surgical cut into her emotions. She learned to compartmentalize, to detach from anything that might weaken her. Feelings were flaws, they told her. She believed them. Even now the echoes of their lessons clung to her, a second skin she couldn't shed. She'd mastered the art of deception, but at the cost of forgetting who she was.

Her memories ran sharp, a blade against her mind. The combat training was brutal, each drill a test of her will. Delia saw the young girl she used to be, battered but determined, pushed beyond her limits until her weakness became strength. They made her fight until her knuckles split, until the world was a blur of pain and determination. She learned to endure, to rise above the hurt, to become someone who never flinched, who never doubted.

Each injury left its mark, evidence of their harsh tutelage. Her transformation was violent, from scared child to efficient operative. But Delia remembered the cost, the long nights of isolation and the way she forced herself not to care. Her past crowded in, vivid and suffocating, pressing against her like a tide that wouldn't recede. She noticed its pull, the struggle to maintain her footing in a life built on lies.

Delia awoke, but the memories persisted. Her eyes moved to the lamp, its unsteady glow a mirror of the facilities that had become her world. It drew her to her darkest memory, the one she fought hardest to forget. Her first kill—they called it a simulation. Delia knew better. She tracked the man's face as she pulled the trigger, the shock in his eyes when he realized it was real. He'd been another recruit, another pawn in their game. They taught her well; they taught her ruthlessness.

She remembered the disbelief, the way her hands shook when it was over. The emotional isolation echoed in those moments, the sense that she was alone in her understanding. The Organization praised her, called it a success, a necessary step. But Delia perceived the shift, the loss of something she couldn't name.

The memories left her raw, a testament to her survival and the cost it exacted. The wound she'd bandaged throbbed in time with the past, a physical reminder of all she'd endured. She looked around the room, the flicker of the lamp casting shadows that stretched like ghosts. She gasped, the memories a gale against everything she held dear.

Delia sagged against the wall, the images crowding her vision giving way to the present. She stood among them, bruised and bleeding but unbroken. The safe house was sparse, but it was hers, for the moment.

They wouldn't defeat her. She'd come too far, lost too much. Delia took another breath, steadying herself for the task ahead. She wouldn't let the past destroy her. Not now. Not ever.

The phone sliced through the silence, a reminder that some ghosts were still alive. Delia hesitated before answering, the name on the display like a murmur of everything she'd tried to leave behind. David. She answered the call, knowing that it couldn't be traced. She knew David didn't know that. The phone and the encryption software were new. She had never mentioned it to him. He was trying to locate her.

His voice spilled through the line. He sounded cheerful. "Hi, babe, I've missed you. How are you?"

The words reached her like an echo of what they'd once had. She imagined his expression, the familiar way he ran a hand through his hair when she disappeared.

"I'm fine," she said, her voice a thin veneer over the truth.

"Any chance you'll be coming home soon? The house is empty without you," he said. "Can you tell me where you are, so I don't have to worry?"

"I'm working on some very tough negotiations for several of my clients. I don't know how long it will take."

"You sound tired. What can I do to help?"

"Nothing. I'm fine," she responded. Her voice was weary.

"We both know you're not. I can hear it in your voice," he said. "Where are you? Maybe I can come to you?"

David, in all their years of marriage, had never pushed her when she was away from home. This was different. She questioned how he knew she was involved. Had he seen her at the compound, or was someone feeding him information? Someone at the embassy.

The distance in David's voice was not just from the phone line but from the years of secrets, every unspoken word, every careful omission that now lay heavy between them.

"Delia, please talk to me," he said, but she caught the shift in his tone: not a plea anymore, but something between a demand and a confession.

She could picture him in the tidy kitchen of their house, pacing with the phone pressed to his ear, one hand knotted in the hem of his shirt. The echo behind him, the faint shuffle of slippers on linoleum, the whine of the refrigerator, grounded her in a world that was suddenly small and foreign. Except she knew he was in Istanbul, and that made her angry.

"Where are you?" he asked.

It was a question she'd never answered directly, not in the hundreds of calls across the years. Delia let the silence fill, measuring how long before he reached for something sharper. She imagined the questions he was rehearsing, the scenarios swirling in his mind.

He was aware of the rules of her world: don't ask, don't linger, don't follow. And now he was trying to get her to answer. She wondered who was listening to their conversation. Most likely the IT techs at the Organization.

She held the phone tighter, afraid her own breath might betray her. Every instinct screamed to sever the connection, to slip beneath the current and disappear for his sake as much as her own. But something in David's voice tethered her. He'd always been the only person who saw through her performances, the only one she allowed behind the mask. He was the only one who made her wish, for a flicker of time, that she could be someone ordinary. Someone who could answer a simple question honestly.

"Don't try to find me," she said, voice flat. "If anyone asks, you don't know where I am or what I'm doing."

His breath caught; she heard it, a microsecond pause that said more than words. "Delia, you can't keep shutting me out," he continued, the edge in his voice a mask for the fear beneath it. "Are you okay?"

Her eyes drifted to the makeshift bandages, the raw edges of her recent past. "I'm fine," Delia repeated, the lie clear to both.

"That's not an answer." His persistence was a mirror of the man she'd fallen for, but it cut deeper now, the reflection distorted by years of deception.

"Then why ask?" she countered, struggling to keep the emotion from her voice.

The line crackled with silence. Delia imagined him on the other end, the clean-cut civil servant with worry lines just forming at the corners of his eyes. She'd traced those lines once, the path of her own happiness.

David's voice broke through again, softer now, but no less insistent. "If you're in danger, I can help."

"In danger from the people you work for," she thought to herself, but she kept silent. He was attempting to gather any tiny bit of information that would give him insight into what she was doing. His pretending made her furious, but she held her temper.

A flicker of longing crossed her features, quickly hidden beneath layers of rehearsed detachment. "I don't need your help," Delia replied, her tone clipped, the professional wall firmly in place.

His laugh was bitter, an echo of shared history and fractured trust. "You always say that. I always know better."

The call was a lifeline and a noose, tightening with every word. Delia held the phone tight, a muscle in her jaw working as she fought the urge to confide, to reach through the static and hold on to what they'd once had, but that was impossible now.

"I know what I'm doing, David."

"Then why does it feel like you're slipping away?" The rawness in his voice cracked her composure, leaving a hairline fracture hard to mend.

Delia took a breath, her silence now a fragile barrier against her feelings for David. She'd built her life on silence, on secrets. This was no different, yet everything was different.

"I miss you," David said, the admission so soft it felt like a confession.

She swallowed hard, her response a ghost of emotion she wouldn't allow. "I have to go," Delia whispered, the finality of her words more for herself than for him.

He didn't stop her, the ache in his voice lingering as the line went dead.

The safe house closed in, its barren walls a reminder of all she'd sacrificed. Delia let the phone slip from her grasp. She'd left him before, more times than she could count. But each departure felt like the first, the cut never healing, always raw.

She turned to the go bag, her movements mechanical, deliberate. The wedding photo lay inside, a snapshot of a life she tried to believe in. Delia's hand hovered over it. The image was too painful to touch.

She picked up the photo and traced the edge with her thumb, brushing over David's face, the connection too real, too immediate. Her breath caught, the vulnerability of the moment threatening to undo her careful defenses.

She placed the photo back, the memory a ghost that refused to be exorcised. The call had stirred more than she could suppress, the reminder of what she'd lost too keen to ignore.

Delia sat back, her body taut with emotions she'd buried under years of assignments and obligations. She felt the ache of absence, the hollow space where David used to be. It left her exposed in ways she swore she'd never allow.

Her jaw clenched against the surge of feeling, the muscle tight beneath her skin. Delia's shoulders tensed, the rigidity a poor substitute for the warmth she'd turned her back on.

The Organization had given her purpose, but it came with a cost. Love was collateral damage, and David was the price she paid. She reminded herself of that, forced the mantra into her mind like a lifeline.

Her breath steadied, each exhale pushing the weakness back into a place where it couldn't touch her. Delia wouldn't let it. She couldn't afford to.

She pulled the bag closer, securing it with the finality of a decision made and remade a thousand times. Her vulnerability was a fleeting bruise, one she pressed down on with the full weight of her need to finish the job.

David was now another one of her ghosts, but Delia refused to be haunted.

Delia's mind caught fire, a blaze that turned grief into grit. Intelligence flooded the table, a jigsaw of deception waiting to be solved. She marked it with ruthless clarity, each piece a spark in the blaze that fueled her. The map transformed into a battle plan: Escape routes. Suspects. Allies. The names of potential moles that she circled in bold ink read like an indictment. David's ghost left her fragile but fierce, the pain now channeled into a singular focus. Find Tommy. Expose the traitor. Her hands were steady, her heart relentless. The plan burned with the heat of her convictions.

The table became her world, every inch covered in the stark reality of her mission. Notes on the syndicate, maps of Istanbul, profiles of the operatives she would need to break. Her analysis was brutal and precise, each movement as calculated as the heart she tried to still. The safe house was filled with her goals, the earlier shadows now banished by the light.

She identified potential locations where Tommy might be held, each one marked with meticulous detail. Her mind wove strategies around them, complex tapestries of risk and rescue.

Safe houses dotted her map like stars in a constellation of survival. Every location a beacon, every line a lifeline.

Delia mapped escape routes with the foresight of a woman who refused to be trapped. Her plans accounted for every variable, every outcome. Timing was everything, and she scheduled the seconds with the confidence of a woman who valued each one. The thoroughness of her work spoke to the shift inside her, from emotional chaos to tactical clarity.

She paused over a list of names: the moles, and the monsters. And now she added one more name to her list: the director, the leader of the Organization that David worked for and that was once her family. She didn't know why they were involved, but if there was money to be made and the stealth fighter plans were worth a significant amount of money, then the Organization would be involved.

She couldn't understand why they would work with someone like Blume, but it was obvious that they were working together. One name glared at her, an accusation she couldn't ignore. Morrison. He was desperate enough, connected enough. She scribbled his name with sharp strokes, the ink bleeding into the paper.

Every possibility explored. Every betrayal expected.

Her phone chimed, and she opened the text from Harper. She had sent him the license plate for the diplomatic SUV, and he had done his homework. She now knew which embassy owned the SUV, and it gave her a place to start to find Tommy.

Delia's hands moved with the grace of conviction, her emotions a focused torrent that pushed her forward. She couldn't allow herself to miss anything, and she didn't. The cost was too high, the stakes too real.

The room filled with the sounds of preparation, the tactical gear readying for the war she'd declared. Weapons gleamed with the hope of protection and retribution. Her equipment needs were calculated, a study in efficiency and power.

As dawn touched the edges of the city, Delia reviewed her intel with the certainty of a final decision. Her motivation was unyielding, the fire inside her burning with new intensity. She had to find Tommy. She had to unmask the traitor. Nothing would stop her.

Her personal pain was a ghost she'd outrun. It fueled her, a secret ally in the battle she was determined to win.

Delia zipped the go bag with a sense of closure that had eluded her for years. She left the wedding photo behind, her eyes lingering on it for a fleeting moment before the mission reclaimed her focus. Tommy's face, David's betrayal, the director's involvement. They all merged into a single path, a single purpose.

She checked her weapons, the feel of them real. A contrast to the doubt that had threatened to undo her. Not anymore. Delia sealed the safe house, every lock a promise to return stronger and closer to the truth.

She stepped out into the awakening city. The world spread before her, a web of danger.

She was ready.

The Double Cross

Delia had slipped into the next safe house, this one across from the Iranian Embassy and another gift from Hamza. This safe house was a small, nondescript apartment with beige walls and a threadbare rug. Delia sat on a folding chair, surrounded by crumpled maps and scattered papers. She settled in to wait until the appointed time. She huddled in the blue glow of the screen, the room stark with photos, maps and the scatter of her mission. The video call connected, and Hamza's face filled the frame. Delia struck first, the accusation sharp and immediate.

"You've been feeding the syndicate," she said. His expression didn't waver, but his voice was cut with steel: denial and then revelation.

"And you've been leaving a trail of bodies across the city. Do you know how hard I must work to protect you?"

He leaned in, the words heavy as gunfire. "I believe James Morrison orchestrated his own son's kidnapping."

The screen cast Delia's features in cool relief, accentuating the conflict that roiled beneath. Hamza's bombshell lingered, shocking her with its audacity. She maintained her composure, but the thought was not a new one. She too believed he was more involved than he was letting on.

"Morrison?" Her voice carried a rare slice of emotion. She studied Hamza's face, searching for a crack in his confidence, a tell that he was bluffing.

His eyes held hers with unyielding intensity. "Morrison has more to gain from this than you realize," he asserted. Each word was deliberate, piercing through her like a finely honed blade.

Delia felt her world shift. She realized deep inside that it was true, but she didn't want to admit it to herself. Her mind raced to catch up, to reconfigure the mission considering this information. It was a familiar yet unwelcome sensation, one that tested the limits of her control.

"Are you certain?" Delia asked, the defiance in her voice undercut by the knowledge in her own head that she couldn't suppress.

Her professional mask cracked, exposing the vulnerability she fought to conceal. If Morrison was playing them all, if Tommy was just a pawn . . . the implications were almost too much to process.

Hamza continued, his expression calculated and intense. "He's using his son's abduction as cover to sell the plans and disappear," he explained, his voice unwavering. "The intel points to him being the one pulling the strings."

Delia's heart pounded, a rapid and unsteady beat that echoed the chaos of her thoughts. She tried to reconcile the image of Morrison, the desperate father she met, with the mastermind Hamza described.

"You have to see how this fits," he pressed, his tone carrying the strength of both command and persuasion. "His access. His connections. It's the only explanation."

Hamza's certainty left little room for argument, but Delia's instincts screamed for more proof. She was torn between the loyalty she felt for Morrison's plight and the undeniable logic of Hamza's words.

"Morrison . . . he's desperate," Delia countered, clinging to the image of the broken man she'd left in the market. "I've seen it. He's terrified for Tommy."

"Desperation makes people dangerous," Hamza replied, his expression softening into something almost paternal. "He's staging this entire operation. You're a critical part of his plan."

The thought landed with the impact of a physical blow. Delia's trust had been a measured calculation, but the possibility of such a deep betrayal left her reeling. She'd been blind to it before. She wouldn't be blind again.

Hamza leaned closer, his presence commanding even through the screen. "Morrison knows your involvement increases his chances of success. He knows how to play you."

The accusation pierced through her defenses, cutting deeper than she would admit. Delia accepted the sting of recognition, the familiar pain of trust turned against her. She had walked this line too many times before, each betrayal a fresh wound.

"He understood that the Organization would try to stop him, and he believed I would stop the Organization if I found out they were involved. But I needed to find that out on my own to make him look legit. He's out to screw the Organization, but he's also planning to screw Blume. Now that Blume has Tommy, everything has changed," she said.

"Precisely," said Hamza. "He was unaware that the Organization wanted the plans for themselves. Once they had the plans, they would join forces with Blume and sell them to his client, the Iranian government."

"Why did you keep me in the dark with this?" she asked.

"We just found out ourselves. The syndicate compound that was attacked last night was a treasure trove of information. The syndicate was brokering a deal with the Iranians. Blume had offered his expert negotiating skills to the syndicate, and they had accepted, having never worked a deal this large before. Blume had a different plan. He invited the Organization to back him in exchange for a much larger piece of the pie. I must say I was stunned when I viewed the video from cameras we had set up on the compound and saw your husband in the mix. I'll bet that was an unpleasant realization."

Her thoughts were a maelstrom, conflicting truths colliding with brutal intensity. Could Morrison have orchestrated such an elaborate deception? The scope of it was staggering, yet Delia couldn't ignore the growing sense that it was true.

She locked eyes with Hamza, the full weight of his conviction settling over her like a shroud. The call's blue glow cast shadows on her face, amplifying the turmoil that churned beneath her calm exterior.

"Can you stop the sale in your official capacity?" she asked.

Hamza smiled. "My government has refused to get involved. We are in the midst of serious negotiations with Iran, and our involvement in stopping this deal could ruin everything. It's up to you to stop this."

"This changes everything," Delia said, the words heavy with the knowledge that they had entered uncharted territory.

The mission was far more complex than she'd imagined, and the risk was greater than she'd expected. Morrison, the Organization, Blume, Tommy, every element was now tinged with suspicion and danger.

Hamza observed her, gauging her reaction with the skill of a master tactician. He could see the shift in her demeanor the moment her doubt turned to grim acceptance. Delia would follow the thread of betrayal, no matter where it led.

His silence spoke volumes, a tacit acknowledgment of the burden he had placed on her shoulders. Delia's focus solidified, the tremor in her hand stilled by the cold certainty of purpose.

She wouldn't let history repeat itself. Not this time. Not with stakes so high and a young man's life in danger.

Delia's demand cut through the silence like a blade. "Send me proof," she said, her skepticism cold and sharp. Hamza leaned back, the screen flickering with calculated intent.

"I'll get you everything I have," he promised, his words a careful gambit. "Two hours, encrypted files, precise coordinates."

The call ended, suspicion and doubt coiling in the empty room. The stillness closed in, the consequence of betrayal as palpable as her breath. It consumed her.

The cold light of the laptop etched Delia's silhouette against the walls, accentuating the tension that pulsed through her. Her mind spun with Hamza's revelation, each turn of thought a spiral of apprehension.

She studied the photos of Morrison and Tommy, each one shadowed by the lingering question of loyalty—or betrayal. Her gaze lingered on the picture of Morrison, his despair and panic, once so convincing, now shaded with suspicion.

The stakes had transformed, the landscape of her mission shifting beneath her. Delia struggled to find solid ground, the full impact of the implications weighing against her chest. She'd been certain of so much, and now it all felt like a lie.

Her thoughts collided, anger and disbelief locking into a tight knot that she couldn't untangle. Was Hamza playing her, spinning a story to see how she'd react? Or was the betrayal as deep and dangerous as he'd suggested?

Delia's breath was shallow, the tension of the call still thrumming. She forced herself to focus, to peel back the layers of deception and see what lay beneath. The sudden silence was both oppressive and clarifying, allowing her to hear the frantic rhythm of her own heartbeat.

The doubts grew louder, each one demanding her attention. She could feel them pulling at her resolve, threatening to undo everything she'd worked to build. She had to stay one step ahead, had to anticipate the next move. Her own ambiguity was the enemy she couldn't face.

As the hours bled into one another, Delia's meticulous review of the intel she had collected so far brought her no closer to the truth. Her instincts warred with logic, creating a battlefield of second guesses. The significance of Hamza's accusation nagged at her, every possibility leading to another set of questions.

She stepped back, surveying the room with a critical eye. The mission had become a web of deceit, each thread leading to another snare. She felt the heaviness of it all, the pressure to unravel the truth before it ensnared her.

The dead drop loomed large, a test of both trust and treachery. She couldn't make any mistakes, couldn't afford to let the Organization or Morrison outmaneuver her. The evidence would hold the answers, or it would lead her further into the trap.

Her hands were steady as she secured the gear, each motion a counterpoint to the ambivalence she felt. Delia's mind focused, hardening into a singular purpose so she could see this through.

But beneath the surface, doubt still gnawed at her. She felt its sharp teeth every time she paused, every time she allowed herself to wonder who was playing whom. The layers of manipulation were endless, each one feeding into her deepest fear: that she was alone in this, that every ally was a phantom, every truth a mirage.

Her thoughts drifted to Harper, one of the few lifelines that hadn't frayed. She hesitated, considering the risk of reaching out, of exposing her one potential ally if Hamza's claims proved true. The temptation was strong, a tether to the stability she craved.

But the danger was too real, too immediate. The situation was too risky, with everything hanging in the balance. Delia forced herself to abandon the idea, to face the reality that she might have to do this on her own.

The decision left her breathless, a flash of vulnerability cutting through her resolve. She shook it off, clinging to the strength that had carried her this far.

Delia sealed the go bag. She was running out of time, running out of trust. The dead drop was four blocks away and with it, the answers she desperately needed.

She wouldn't let doubt destroy her. Not again.

Race Against Time

The laptop glowed in the dim hotel room, casting Delia's fingers in frenetic shadow as she set the bait. False intel. Breadcrumbs for a traitor. She uploaded the files, just as Harper had instructed, watching her deception take shape. What she was planning settled on her shoulders, but she bore it with strength. The tablet also displayed the facility's schematics, each detail searing into her brain with the critical need for survival. Tommy's frightened face lingered in her memory.

She had reviewed the information Hamza had provided at the dead drop. Everything pointed to Morrison as the betrayer, staging his son's kidnapping to enrich himself after years of toiling in silence for the government.

The files showed a compulsive gambler and drinker. A man deep in debt who needed a big win to get out from under his cloud. He had set up escape routes for himself, his wife and Tommy, with the help of friends from the time he spent working in the field. The stealth plans were where he needed them. All that was left was getting them.

The information showed that Blume would act as his go-between for the sale to the Iranians. Secret bank accounts had already been set up all around the world. Transfers were ready, waiting for the sale to complete.

Delia realized two things after reading the files. Blume was playing for every team. He had helped the local syndicate with setting up the network to force Morrison to get them the plans to sell to the Iranians, and then he had his personal army attack the compound and kill every member of the syndicate. Now he was working with the Organization, clearing the way for them to get their hands on the fighter plans so they could sell them to the Iranians with his help.

She wondered at what point he was going to betray them. And the information she received from Hamza showed Morrison as the ringleader behind all the betrayals, so he could sell the plans to the Iranians for his own benefit. From everything Delia had learned, the sure bet was that Blume would be very wealthy when all was said and done. And in the end, she would find that the Iranian government was behind the plan.

Delia had thought long and hard about the information Hamza had delivered to her, and she had come to one conclusion. She did not believe Morrison was behind the sale. It was true that all roads led to Morrison, but it was all too pat, too perfect. She had sat with Morrison in their first meeting and had looked deep into his soul.

One thing that was important in Delia's job was the ability to read people, and what she observed during that first meeting was a man who was distraught and fearful. She was aware people could fake many things, but the emotions she felt from Morrison were real. She believed it then, and she still believed it now, no matter what the files showed. She believed the information Hamza had received was contrived, and she hoped that by accessing the files at the Iranian embassy, she could prove his innocence and unveil the true mole.

The lines of text blurred then sharpened as Delia double-checked the intel she was about to upload to the USB drive Harper had prepared for her. Every piece was just credible enough to tempt, yet pointed to the same explosive conclusion.

The stealth fighter plans were buried where no one would find them. She leaned back, the chair creaking beneath her, and let out a breath she didn't realize she was holding.

The deception was a heavy load. The danger of exposure was real. But Delia had to wear it, had to make the stakes clear enough that the mole couldn't resist taking the bait. Her fingers lingered over the keyboard before shutting the tablet. In the quiet that followed, she moved with renewed purpose, each action precise and deliberate.

She slipped into her black pants and shirt, black soft-soled shoes completing the outfit. She unholstered her silenced pistol; the weight felt reassuring in her hand. She tested the magazine, slid it back into place with a soft click. She did the same with her knives, making sure they were accessible when the time came. Delia worked with focus. She thrived on preparation, each task a thread she wove into the larger fabric.

The last piece was Harper's contribution, the specialized USB drive that would breach the compound's computers if her intel was as good as she believed. She packed it all into a compact go bag, securing it with methodical care.

Her mind wandered to Tommy as she worked, to the scared boy she had seen as David and Blume walked him to the waiting SUV, his head covered, and to the promise she'd made to bring him home. The image spurred her on, an engine that drove her to continue even when doubt nipped at her heels.

What she was about to do weighed on her, but Delia was used to this kind of pressure, used to turning it into an ally rather than an enemy. She opened her phone, the screen's light slicing through the gloom with sharp and welcome focus.

The facility's schematics that she had transferred from Harper's tablet glowed back at her. Delia absorbed each piece with the intensity of a person who grasped the cost of failure. She flicked through guard rotations, security protocols, the placement of every surveillance camera. Her breath quickened with anticipation rather than fear, each new piece of information a crucial addition to her arsenal.

Her eyes scanned the phone, lingering on the live image from a security camera overlooking the server room. She pondered how Harper had gained access to the cameras. The shot was grainy but unmistakable. She placed her phone in her back pocket. She was as ready as she'd ever be.

Delia set the tablet down, the glow diminishing as she switched it off. The room plunged back into dimness, the shadows familiar and unthreatening. They felt like companions, like comrades, the allies she could trust.

Her preparations complete, Delia paused, letting the magnitude of what lay ahead settle over her. She would hit the facility with everything she had, and when the mole took the bait, she'd be waiting. Delia grabbed the go bag, its weight a reminder of what she was about to do. She took one last look around the room, ensuring she'd left no trace of herself. Then she headed into the night, the bait ready and the mission burned into her memory.

The Iranian Embassy crouched like a beast, razor wire topping the wrought iron fence that surrounded the property. Security lights glinted like teeth. Delia dodged the shadows, her presence a whisper against the backdrop of concrete and silence. She timed her approach with clinical precision, each guard's movement memorized, every move a calculated risk.

At the perimeter, she was liquid grace. She stopped at the maintenance door and used her picks to unlock the door. She pulled out her phone, set it next to the alarm panel and clicked the keys. The red light on the alarm panel flashed and then turned green. She pulled open the door and entered the building, quiet as a church mouse.

The fluorescent lights in the hallway cast everything in a harsh, sterile glow, but Delia moved like a spirit. Every shift of her body was intentional, every breath controlled and silent.

Inside, the embassy unfolded like a maze, each hallway a calculated trap. Delia treaded softly, the soles of her shoes making no sound on the industrial flooring. Her path was a delicate balance of caution and speed as she navigated the narrow space between urgency and stealth.

She crouched low, the lines of her black suit blending seamlessly with the shadows. The corridors stretched ahead in long, sterile lines. The building was empty except for a skeleton crew of maintenance and cleaning personnel and the guards. She paused, listening to the facility's mechanical hum and the distant shuffle of guards.

Delia moved, swift and assured, a ghost against the harshness of the fluorescent lights. She calculated each move, a dancer in a deadly performance where even the smallest mistake could spell failure. Her instincts guided her. A lifetime of training compressed into each second, each step.

Delia could make out the smell of cleaning chemicals as the overnight crew prepared the embassy for the next day's business. The smell was antiseptic and reminded her of a recent hospital stay. Delia welcomed the discomfort; it kept her alert, every sense tuned to the mission's plan.

She froze in a doorway, her breath a slow, rhythmic beat. A guard passed, unaware of her presence, his shadow long and looming before it faded into nothingness. Delia counted to three, then moved again, her pace doubling as she raced through the building.

Security cameras dotted the ceilings like vigilant eyes, but Harper's intel had given her every angle, every blind spot. Delia ducked beneath them, a shadow among shadows. The building was a predator's lair, and she moved within it as if she had no fear.

Her pulse quickened as she neared her destination, the reality of her presence in the heart of enemy territory pushing adrenaline into her veins.

The server room door, the massive slab of reinforced metal, was the last barrier between her and the mission's critical moment.

The mechanism was complex, but she'd tackled worse. She approached the digital panel next to the door. She touched the screen, and a blue light appeared. She checked her phone and entered a series of numbers, and the panel glowed green. She opened an app and uploaded a retinal scan that Harper had provided. She had no idea how he got the scan data. With the upload complete, she held her phone in front of the scanner and watched as red lines moved in several directions. The lines stopped, and there were a few seconds of tension before she heard the lockset click.

The handle turned beneath her palm. Delia took a breath, her fingers hesitating for a second before she pushed the door wide.

Red lights pulsed in the dark, a rhythmic glow that seemed to match the beat of her heart. The server room stretched before her, rows of humming machines casting the space in cool illumination. She stepped inside, the sound enveloping her in a promise and a challenge. It had been a long time since she had been in such a room, but this one seemed large compared to the ones in her memories. She contemplated how much of the server space was devoted to eavesdropping and spying on the other embassies and government agencies that populated the area.

Delia scanned the rows, looking for the server number Harper had provided. She found the correct row and moved down the line until she spotted the server. She pulled the USB drive out of her backpack and opened the server cover, inserting the drive into the slot. Her plan was about to come to fruition.

The servers hummed a digital symphony, each note a promise of deception. Delia connected the USB drive, slid out the keyboard from its place on the server and turned it on. The screen above the server lit up with a green tint. Her fingers were a blur on the keyboard.

The download progress bar crawled in slow motion; each percentage completed seemed like an eternity. Sweat beaded on her brow, her focus sharp and unyielding. The green light on the USB drive turned to red, and she entered the final codes Harper had given her. The server hummed as it absorbed this new information.

Delia pulled out the drive and placed it in her backpack. She pulled a second drive out of her back pocket and slipped it into the slot. This would be her payment to Harper for his help. She was now at the intel-gathering portion of their plan. A price she was willing to pay for his help.

The red light on the end of the drive flashed, and she entered the codes into the keyboard. Red lights along the bank of servers started flashing, and the hum in the room increased. She was glad Harper had warned her that this would happen, or she might have grabbed her gear and bolted.

She followed the commands on the small screen, her fingers flying across the keyboard, each stroke unlocking the server's secrets. Delia willed the progress bar to move faster, every second a spike of tension that drove into her nerves. The digital clock ticked louder in her mind, a metronome of risk. The light on the USB turned green, and she replaced the keyboard.

An alarm blared, a banshee wail. Red lights flashed. Delia didn't know what had set off the alarms, but she was not going to wait around to find out. She snatched the drive from the server slot. She heard the facility locking down around her with hisses and clicks. Doors sealed, a metal confession of her presence.

The red emergency lights transformed the room into a surreal landscape, casting long shadows that danced with the pressing need to escape. Delia sensed the entire compound's attention swing towards her, the full focus of their security now an immediate and deadly threat.

She pressed ahead, adrenaline honing her senses to a razor's edge. The pneumatic hiss of sealing doors echoed through the facility, a cold metallic whisper that threatened to trap her. Delia darted for the sealed door, pulled out her phone and held it next to the access panel. The red light turned green, and the door released. She pushed open the door a crack and checked the corridor. She opened the door and moved towards the egress point she had memorized.

The two guards appeared out of nowhere, their weapons trained on her with unwavering precision. But Delia was faster, her training second nature requiring no thought, just action.

Her footwork was precise, a dance of evasion and attack that left no room for error. She deflected the first guard's aim with a fluid strike, the movement seamless as she redirected his momentum into a collision with his partner.

The second guard stumbled, his defenses shattered by the impact. Delia was on them both, her strikes a blur of efficiency that left no time for recovery. She disarmed the first guard with a twist that sent his weapon skittering across the floor, her control absolute. A blow to the side of his head ended his part in the fight. The second guard pushed himself off the ground. A devastating knee to the solar plexus and an elbow to the temple took the fight out of the guard.

Both guards lay motionless, their bodies slack and unresponsive. Delia stood over the unconscious men, her breath little changed by the effort, her heartbeat slow and steady. They were both lucky that Delia was not interested in leaving any dead bodies in her wake.

More footsteps approached, snapping her back into motion. She calculated her escape, the options narrowing as the compound's forces converged on her position. The corridor stretched ahead, a canyon of risk that demanded everything she had.

Delia darted down the hallway, the red lights still pulsing a relentless warning, the sirens wailing. She counted the seconds, her internal clock as precise as the digital ones. There was no room for doubt, no room for hesitation. With guards closing in from both ends, Delia made a split-second decision. She veered left, the maintenance chute a narrow promise of escape.

The cover was tight, claustrophobic, but it was enough. Delia ducked inside, the metal cool against her skin. The sound of pursuit faded, replaced by the echo of her heartbeat and the distant thrum of the facility's alarms. She slid down the shaft and landed in the maintenance area, a large trash bin softening her landing.

Delia paused just long enough to catch her breath, to reorient herself in the labyrinth she'd entered. The drive was safe in her pocket, the download complete. But she recognized that this was just the beginning. Delia needed to move, the path ahead a maze of deception. She was ready for whatever came her way.

The maintenance tunnels squeezed tight around her, each turn a chokehold of risk. Delia moved quickly. Heavy footsteps and shouted commands echoed, urgency made real by proximity. She slipped through a door and scanned the hallway ahead. She emerged into another wing of the compound. Blume's men were waiting for the intruder to appear.

"We've got him," one said into his radio.

With all the excitement, they still didn't realize Delia was a woman. Delia stepped into the hall, catching the men by surprise. She fired twice, her silenced pistol a lethal whisper. She took their radio and ran, the facility a hive of pursuit.

Delia stepped into a room labeled fire command center in several languages. She opened the control panel and ran her finger along the buttons and switches. She found the toggle she was looking for and switched it on. Sprinklers erupted overhead, her diversion buying time. Running through the downpour, Delia raced towards the loading dock.

She heard the shouts, the pounding of boots on wet concrete, and she pushed herself harder, the urgency driving her faster. The riskiness of each twist and turn didn't slow her; it propelled her with the desperate force of necessity.

Delia burst into the open, the corridor a stark contrast to the confinement she'd just escaped. The fluorescent lights washed everything in a harsh glow, the shadows long and sharp. The presence of Blume's men confirmed what she'd feared and hoped.

Their faces were cold with intent; they were pawns in a game she now understood. The mole was real, and he was closer than she'd let herself believe. Delia moved without hesitation, the silenced shots a soft, deadly punctuation. Her breath steadied as two more men fell.

The radio Delia had taken from the first guard was a tether to the enemy, each transmission a warning and a map. Delia placed the earpiece in her ear and clipped the radio to her belt, listening to the chatter on the radio to guide her past the roadblocks.

The voices on the radio were frantic, the realization of her escape pushing them to recklessness. "The intruder is on the move. We have men down," one reported. Delia didn't let it slow her; she fed off the knowledge, the confirmation that she was a step ahead.

The guards swarmed around her, a hive of pursuit that buzzed with the collective will to catch her. Delia was the variable, the wild card in a hand they thought they'd stacked against her. She was relentless, pushing through the facility with the power of certainty, the drive to survive and succeed a single, burning flame. Her body moved by instinct, every fiber tuned to the need to escape.

Water continued to rain down, the cold shock of it adding to the pandemonium. Alarms screamed anew, the red lights now a strobing backdrop to rushing water and shouts. Delia moved through the chaos, invisible in the blinding panic.

A voice came over the radio, speaking Farsi. "Someone go to the sprinkler room and turn off the damn sprinklers." Delia translated in her head.

The diversion worked, the disarray creating a break in the tightening net. Security guards and Blume's men stumbled through the confusion, their pursuit splintered by the sudden turn of events.

Delia felt the ground tilt in her favor, the danger lifting as she outran their desperate attempts to close the gap. The loading dock came into view, a final gauntlet between her and freedom.

The trucks were lined up, the chance to slip away. Delia sprinted towards them, every step a calculated risk. The water made the ground slick, each footfall a potential fall, a potential end. But she didn't falter, didn't doubt. The mission was too real, too vital. Tommy's face burned in her mind, an ember that pushed her harder and faster.

The alarms and shouts receded as she leaped for the cover of a departing truck. Her body hit the ground and rolled, but Delia was back on her feet, relentless.

The radio she'd taken still crackled with commands, but the urgency had shifted. She was ahead of them, a shadow they couldn't catch. Delia pushed ahead, every part of her alive with the thrill of escape and the expectation of what was yet to come.

She slid beneath a departing trash truck, a desperate shadow clinging to the metal frame. The engine's heat threatened to burn her, the vibrations an assault on her senses. She held on, a tenacious ghost. The truck cleared the guardhouse and passed through the gate.

The guards who were concerned with people breaking into the embassy never checked under the truck for someone trying to escape the embassy. Once clear of the compound, Delia dropped from the vehicle, rolling onto the wet road.

Rain poured down, but she was so wet already it didn't matter. Pain erupted as she hit the ground, but that didn't stop her. She sprinted for the darkness of a nearby alley and stopped to catch her breath. She touched the drive in her pocket, the files she had uploaded more vital than anything. Alarms faded as she escaped, each step a defiant promise to survive.

Her body ached with each movement. The impact of the drop from the moving truck had sent shock waves of pain through her limbs. But Delia pushed through it, the mission a balm against the hurt. She couldn't risk slowing down, couldn't let anything stop her now.

The embassy was behind her, its lights a distant constellation of fury and confusion. The night stretched ahead, a road that promised both freedom and the unknown. Delia proceeded with the determination of someone who'd cheated fate too many times to count.

City streets rose around her, an urban labyrinth that swallowed her whole. She heard sirens heading for the embassy, their cries muffled by distance. Delia escaped the shadows, a hint of defiance in the wet and gleaming dark.

The clandestine meeting place with Harper loomed ahead, the abandoned warehouse a refuge in the maze. She pushed towards it, every step an act of will. The cold rain soaked through her clothes, but she welcomed it, letting it wash away the heat of the escape.

The warehouse offered a stark shelter, empty but dry. Delia secured the door behind her, the final click of the lock a punctuation of success. She pulled out her pistol and moved into the building, the adrenaline of escape still coursing through her veins.

She allowed herself a moment of grim satisfaction, the knowledge that she'd outmaneuvered them a fierce comfort in the desolate space. The facility was in chaos, the bait ready and waiting. The mole would reveal himself, and she'd be there to see it.

She entered a large space and spotted Harper through the dim light cast on the floor from the streetlights outside. He turned and stared at the gun as she approached.

"Are we safe?" asked Delia.

Harper nodded. "No one followed me. From the sounds in the distance, it would appear you succeeded."

Delia smiled through the wet hair hanging in her face. She reached into her back pocket, pulled out the USB drive and handed it to him. He stepped over to an old barrel, pulled his laptop out of his backpack and placed it on the lid. He opened it, clicked a few keys and inserted the drive. His laptop came alive as file after file filled his screen. His expression reminded Delia of a child opening gifts at Christmas.

"Is it what you wanted?" she asked.

He turned. "That and so much more. This will take weeks for us to unravel, but oh my god did we hit the treasure trove." He clicked some keys, pulled out the drive and closed his laptop.

He reached next to the barrel and picked up Delia's go bag.

"I picked this up from the hotel. Thought you might need it." He smiled at her. "I need to get this to my team. We will need to get the NSA and CIA involved, because we don't have the computer power available here. You did great, Delia. I hope the information you left them will lead to what you need."

Harper put his laptop in his backpack, smiled and raced to the door, like a kid with a new toy.

Delia changed into dry clothes she pulled from her bag. She felt the ache of her earlier effort but understood that it was worth it, knew it was a small price for the advantage she'd gained. The drive was safe, the stealth fighter plans moved and secure, thanks to Harper, and the information to expose the mole waiting.

Delia grabbed her bags and left the warehouse. She ran two blocks and grabbed a cab back to her hotel. She was running out of time, but what she had accomplished tonight was worth the time it had taken.

Betrayal Unveiled

Blume's body entwined with Jennifer Morrison's, their breaths syncing in a dance as old as time. Her dark hair covered the pillow, and she moved under him. The sheets beneath them were a twisted, forgotten mess, evidence of the intensity of their passion. Jennifer's fingers traced the muscles of his back, her eyes gleaming with lust and calculation.

"You sure about this, Blume?" she whispered, her voice a husky purr. "The Organization won't take this lightly."

Blume paused, his lips brushing against her neck. "We've been over this, Jen. It's what we've talked about since the beginning. We never intended to share the plans with the Organization. Once we have them in our hands, we'll kill the Organization people just like we did the syndicate."

"But what if the Iranians find out that you betrayed the seller?" she asked, her body pressing against his.

Blume laughed. "All the Iranians know is that I represent the seller. I've never told them who the seller is. They have no idea that you are the actual seller. By the time anyone is wiser, we will be long gone, with a big fat bank account and the world at our fingertips."

She arched against him, stretching her five-foot-nine body against his. Her nipples responded to his soft kisses. A soft moan escaped her lips. "What about the boy? He's going to be caught in the crossfire."

Blume pulled back, his eyes searching hers. "You said you didn't care about him. He's not your son, Jen. He's from James's first marriage. He will be collateral damage, just like his father.

All the evidence you planted will keep James in the spotlight as the traitor. His son will be better off dead than to have to live with the guilt of his father's treachery."

Jennifer's expression hardened, her nails digging into his flesh. "You are an evil man, Mr. Blume, but I worry it will look bad if he gets hurt. We need to be smart about this."

Blume nodded, his hand cupping her cheek. "We will be. He will just become another sad victim, killed during a rescue attempt. We get the stealth fighter plans, sell them to the Iranians and we vanish. No one will know it was us."

Jennifer smiled, a slow, seductive curve of her lips. "You make it sound so easy."

Blume grinned, his body moving against hers in a rhythm that promised more than just conversation. "With you by my side, Jen, anything is possible."

Their bodies moved in tandem, their lovemaking a reflection of their shared ambition. The room filled with their whispered plans and heated breaths; the air was thick with desire and deception. The stealth fighter plans hung over them, a tantalizing reward for their betrayal.

As they reached the peak of their passion, Jennifer's eyes locked with Blume's, a silent pact passing between them. They were in this together, bound by their shared desire for freedom and the thrill of the double cross. The world outside faded away, leaving the two of them and the dangerous game they were playing. The risks were high, but the reward was within reach. And they were ready to claim it, no matter the cost.

Jennifer climbed off Blume and sat on the side of the bed, sipping from a glass of wine. "I plan to retrieve the plans today," she said. "Make sure the Iranians are ready."

Blume pulled her back, spilling wine on her breasts and abdomen, which he licked off.

***

Deception turned to revelation as Harper cracked the first layers of secrecy. Delia moved like a restless thought, her steps marking time against the tap of keys. The room was a storm of shadows and light, each flash from the screen a promise. The electronics sang a constant hymn of discovery, their blue glow casting urgency across their faces.

Rain tattooed the windows, the city's breath misting against the glass. Harper's brow furrowed, his frown an unspoken worry. The words were emerging now, jagged on the screen: Package. Payment. Morrison. Blume. Delia felt her heart in her throat.

Harper worked with skilled focus, his fingers a blur as they flew over the keys. Each keystroke cut through the tension, bringing them closer to understanding. The new safe house was a stark contrast to the bustling city outside. It was dimly lit, with a single bulb hanging from the ceiling casting a yellow glow over the bare walls. The room was sparsely furnished, with a simple cot pushed against one wall and a small desk in the corner.

Delia's presence filled the space, her pacing a sharp counterpoint to Harper's steady focus. She glanced at the screen, then the door, her nerves visible in the way she clenched and unclenched her fists.

Rain lashed the windows, a steady rhythm that echoed the importance of their task. Harper's concentration never wavered, but the flicker of concern on his face was undeniable. Each decoded word revealed more details about the conspiracy, and each revelation added new layers of complexity to the situation.

The messages came into focus, bits of jagged text forming a damning picture. Delia's eyes narrowed as she scanned the screen. **Package secured**, one message read. **Payment on delivery**, said another. The implications were explosive, each line a jolt that reverberated through her.

Harper paused, a brief hesitation that spoke volumes. "It looks like everything you were told about Morrison is true," he said, disbelief in his voice. "I wouldn't have believed it. Morrison has been a stand-up agent for years. I guess he couldn't adjust to being pulled from the field."

As more messages appeared, the evidence was undeniable. Communications between Morrison and Blume, each one colder and more calculated than the last. Delia sensed the floor shift beneath her, the enormity of what they were uncovering threatening to swallow her whole. She hadn't wanted to believe it, but here was the evidence. She wondered how she had not seen it, refused to accept it. She felt like she was losing her skills.

She forced herself to focus, to push past the anger and disbelief that clouded her thoughts. Harper glanced at her, his expression a blend of dread and determination. They were close to the truth, but the closer they got, the more dangerous it became.

Rain continued its relentless dance against the windows, the sound merging with the occasional burst of static from their devices. Delia felt each drop like a countdown, a measure of the time they had left to act. Harper's brow furrowed deeper, their discovery settling over them both like a shroud.

The room pulsed with tension, the low hum of electronics a constant echo of the mission's urgency. Delia stopped pacing, her attention locked on the screen as the last pieces fell into place. Morrison. Blume. Package. Payment. Each word was a knife, cutting away her last shred of doubt.

Harper looked up, his expression one of shock and sadness. "It's worse than we thought," he whispered. Delia's breath caught, her mind racing to connect the dots of betrayal. She had never imagined the extent of Morrison's deceit, but the truth was now undeniably clear.

Morrison's plan was as calculated as it was brutal. He'd sold his soul, and his son, for money. Delia's rage surged, volcanic and immediate, hardening into a chilling admission. She would not let him win.

The scope of it left her reeling. Morrison had orchestrated his own son's kidnapping, using Tommy as a smoke screen for his defection. The dates, the meeting locations, the sterile way he referred to the boy—it all pointed to a monstrous deception.

Delia's jaw clenched as the full story came into focus, each message a bullet point in Morrison's cold, transactional betrayal. The schedule of payments and the exchange of plans confirmed everything. He intended to disappear with the fighter schematics, leaving nothing but collateral damage in his wake.

Delia gripped the table, her knuckles white with the force of her emotion. The realization was a physical blow, and she absorbed it with a mixture of fury and disbelief. Harper remained seated, his silence a stark contrast to the tumult that raged within her. His eyes were wide, the shock of their discovery leaving him momentarily paralyzed. Delia's world had narrowed to the scope of Morrison's treachery, the implications more personal and devastating than she could have imagined.

A chair clattered to the floor as Delia stood abruptly, the noise like a gunshot in the charged air. Her movements were sharp and full of purpose, a violent shift from the detachment she'd clung to. She viewed the screen, her eyes hardening as each message seared into her mind. Morrison's betrayal was complete, his intentions laid bare with brutal clarity. He had treated his own son as a pawn, a disposable asset in a game where the stakes were life and death.

Her heart pounded. Harper's hands hovered over the keyboard, his earlier confidence shattered by what they'd uncovered.

Delia's gaze fell to a photograph that slipped from the file, fluttering to the floor like a wounded bird. Tommy's face stared back at her, innocent and trusting, the starkness of his situation tearing at the last of her defenses.

"I'm going to get that boy back," Delia said, her voice firm. "And Morrison will pay for using his own son like this." The statement was a vow, every syllable weighted with the assurance of action.

Harper's eyes locked on hers, the disbelief in his expression giving way to understanding. Delia had transformed before his eyes, the shift from professional detachment to personal investment as sudden as it was complete. She squared her shoulders, the set of her jaw more determined than he'd ever seen.

The room felt small around them, the tension pushing at the walls like a living thing. Delia absorbed it all—the betrayal, the anger, the need for justice—and let it shape her next move. Her eyes never left the photograph, the focus of her mission now more clear than ever.

The moment stretched, charged with the energy of their discovery and the implications it carried. Delia's movements were deliberate as she gathered the files, each action underscored by a resolve that had taken root in the raw soil of her emotions.

Harper found his voice, the sound tentative against what they'd learned. "Delia, are you sure?" he asked, the question a blend of concern and disbelief.

She met his gaze, the fire in her eyes unquenchable. "He's no better than Blume," she said, the comparison a damning indictment of Morrison's character. "They're all going to pay."

Harper nodded, the gesture heavy with the understanding of the path she'd committed to. She wouldn't let them destroy another life, wouldn't let Tommy become a casualty of Morrison's greed.

The rain continued to beat against the windows, each drop a testament to the urgency of their mission. Delia felt it, the rhythm a counterpoint to the plans she was already forming.

Harper eyed her, the transformation leaving him momentarily speechless. Delia's intensity was a force of nature, the same unyielding determination that had seen her through so much. He knew that she wouldn't stop. That she wouldn't rest until she'd made good on her vow.

Delia acted with conviction, the deliberate, methodical precision showing she recognized what was at stake. Her shoulders squared, her eyes sharp. She was already two steps ahead.

The betrayal had shaken her. It had strengthened her: more dedicated, more dangerous. Delia experienced the shift, the transformation complete and irrevocable. She would get Tommy back, and she would make Morrison pay. Nothing would stop her. Not now. Not ever.

Harper's fingers continued their relentless quest for information. He was about to move on to another file when a thought occurred to him. He opened another program, and he clicked the keys. His frantic rhythm caught Delia's attention, and she stepped behind him to see what he was working on. She watched as the information flooded past her eyes. Harper stopped and faced her.

"I can't figure it out," he said, clicking a few more keys.

Delia pulled over a chair and sat next to him. "What can't you figure out?" she asked.

"I can't figure out how Morrison was going to do it. According to the access files, Morrison doesn't have the clearance to open the files for the stealth fighter. They are cleared way above his rating."

"Couldn't he steal someone's password and open the files that way?" asked Delia.

Harper shook his head. She felt stupid asking such a question, even though she didn't know it was wrong.

"The files are a special category. They're protected by four-level encryption," he said.

"And?" she asked.

"A password is required just to get into the server, but there are also three other levels of random numbers that are generated by the system and assigned randomly to all the folks with access. It would take a miracle for him to figure out the numbers, which can be anywhere from ten to one hundred and fifty digits long."

"Well," said Delia. "How were you able to move the file last night?"

"I have senior admin privileges and way above top-secret clearance, but once I entered the system, it scrambled all my encryption codes and sent new ones to a secure folder in another server. A server that my boss and those of us with the proper clearance can enter and secure the new codes after going through a three-step identification challenge."

Delia looked at him. "Morrison doesn't have that kind of clearance or that kind of knowledge, does he?"

"Not unless he's a programmer of the highest order, and his background doesn't suggest that. As a field agent, he was a low-level user," said Harper. "I just checked, and his password hasn't been changed in years, even though protocol dictates every ninety days."

"Who would have that kind of access besides you?" asked Delia.

"Any programmer with my clearance, or my boss."

"How many people are we talking?" she asked.

"Four, maybe five at the most."

"Do any of these people have connections to James?" asked Delia.

Harper accessed a new server and spent a few minutes going through personnel files, cross-referencing names with James Morrison. He sat back and scratched his head.

"What?" asked Delia.

He hesitated. "My boss," he said.

"What about your boss?" asked Delia.

"My boss is married to James Morrison." He pushed back in his chair. "Holy shit."

"You didn't know this?" said Delia, her glare unmistakable.

"No," he said. "Her name is Jennifer McKenna. She doesn't use her married name at the embassy. There's also no mention of it in her personnel file. I found it in an unclassified payroll file. The addresses match."

Delia scowled. "Get on the internet and find out everything you can about Jennifer Morrison, née McKenna."

Maybe Delia wasn't wrong after all. Maybe she hadn't misjudged Morrison.

The Final Gambit

Jennifer Morrison pressed her fingertips against the embassy's biometric console, heart pounding as the red lines crossed her hand. She waited for what seemed like an eternity before the console changed from red to green and she gained access to the secure computer station. She sat at the lone desk, pulled over the keyboard and entered her access information. The screen came to life.

Jennifer's eidetic memory made remembering the long sequences of numbers easy as she began the four-level encryption process that would get her access to the Department of Defense program containing the documents for the stealth fighter. Her fingers moved across the keyboard as she entered each sequence. She entered the final set of numbers, then sat back and waited. Her screen blinked, then went blank.

A series of file folders appeared, and she clicked on the first one. The file opened but was empty. She knew this wasn't right because she had checked the file two weeks before so she could let Blume know to set up the deal. She clicked on the other folders in the file. All of them were empty.

The stealth fighter blueprints she'd risked everything for were gone. She stared at the empty directory and swallowed hard. Someone had moved the file, and she had no way to know where to look for them. She cursed the world around her, shut down the computer and left the room.

Jennifer didn't stop at her desk; she just breezed through the embassy, ran down the stairs and passed through the security gate. She hailed a cab and gave the driver the address. She sat back, and her body shook.

The cab pulled to a stop at a glass-and-steel skyscraper. Jennifer handed the driver a fistful of cash and bolted from the cab. She ran into the lobby and entered her passcode for the penthouse, and the elevator opened.

Two minutes later, she burst through the door of Blume's penthouse apartment. He was sitting by the floor-to-ceiling windows overlooking the streets of Istanbul and was eating a late lunch. As soon as Jennifer ran into the room, he saw the distress on her face.

"The file is missing," she said, her voice higher pitched than she expected.

Blume stared at her. He set down his glass. "What do you mean it's missing?" He stood and approached her. "You lost it?" he demanded before she could speak.

She glared at him. "It's gone. Empty."

Blume stopped, his jaw tight. "Who would do that?" He ran a hand through his hair. "We have four hours before the Iranians show up. What the fuck are we supposed to do? No file, no deal." His hands shook, and his face got red. "Can't you find it?"

She glared at him incredulously. "Don't you think if I could have found it, I would have? What a fucking stupid question."

They circled each other, words sharp as blades. Blume's knuckles whitened around his whiskey glass. "If we walk in empty-handed, they kill us on the spot."

Jennifer's eyes blazed. "Do you think I don't fucking know that?"

Blume stopped and controlled his breathing. "I think we still can go through with the deal."

"What the fuck are you talking about?" asked Jennifer. "That file could be anywhere. There's no way I could find it in time for the meeting."

"We don't need the file." He reached out and took her by the arms and led her to the couch. They sat, and he smiled at her. "Look. We were going to kill the folks from the Organization at the meeting and then deal directly with the Iranians. So now we also kill the Iranians, but we keep alive whichever guy has the laptop, force him to transfer the funds and then we kill him."

"What about Tommy?" she asked.

"Kill him or keep him alive. It won't matter. His father will be dead no matter what, and all the blame will fall on him. Either way, the kid is parentless."

"Where is James?" she asked.

"I sent some of my boys to pick him up. Just waiting for a call that they have him. All the pieces are falling into place. In a few hours, we will be rich and on my jet to Saudi Arabia. From there, we can go anywhere."

The silence stretched. Then Jennifer nodded once, cold acceptance in her gaze. "Agreed. We eliminate everyone at the airstrip and disappear with the money. No one will ever find us."

Blume smiled. "I need to call the boys and have them get to the airport to prepare."

Blume checked his pistol under the couch cushion. Jennifer unholstered her weapon beneath her jacket, her breathing slow, her mind laser-focused. Outside, the city pulsed, unaware of the storm about to break in its neon streets.

Blume moved to the table and poured two glasses of champagne. He handed one to Jennifer. "To us."

They clinked glasses, and Jennifer raised her silenced pistol and shot him in the head. He fell onto the table, and the champagne spilled onto the floor.

***

Harper watched as Jennifer walked out of the secure computer room and made her way towards the door. He pulled out his phone and dialed.

"She's on the move, and she does not look happy," he said.

"Good," said Delia. "Any sign of Morrison at the embassy? I've been trying to reach him, but he's not picking up."

Harper pulled up the access log on his laptop and ran down the list. "He hasn't passed through security today. He must have stayed home."

"Okay. Let me know if he shows. I'm gonna follow our friend Jennifer."

"Good luck, Delia," he said. The call disconnected.

Delia hailed a cab and followed Jennifer to a high-rise apartment building in the heart of downtown. She observed as Jennifer exited the cab, walked into the building, entered a code and stepped into the elevator. Delia slid out of the cab and waited. Once the elevator door closed, Delia walked into the lobby and approached the security screen. She entered Jennifer McKenna in the search bar and found nothing. She entered

Gerhardt Blume in the search bar, and after a few seconds his name appeared on the screen.

"Wow, the penthouse. Not bad, Blume," she said with a laugh.

She pulled out her phone and held it next to the panel. She opened an app and entered a command. A few seconds went by, then the panel announced her passcode was accepted and she entered the elevator. She stopped the elevator one floor below the penthouse and exited, moving down the hall until she found the fire exit.

She opened the door and looked into the stark stairwell. She took the stairs two at a time and stopped at the penthouse door. She used her phone on the control panel, which was just like the one in the lobby, and pulled open the door. She pulled her pistol from her holster and closed the door.

Delia could hear yelling deeper in the apartment. She slid behind the bar and listened, arriving just as Blume laid out his plan to screw everyone. She heard them clink glasses and was surprised when she heard the silenced poof from a pistol and heard someone crash onto a table. She held her position, pistol at the ready.

Jennifer's footsteps moved across the hardwood, quick and determined. Delia tracked her with the accuracy of a hunter, every sense attuned to the slightest change. She waited until the elevator door closed, then moved from her cover and stepped into the room, her weapon leading the way.

The sight of Blume's body was a grim confirmation. Blood pooled beneath him, mingling with the champagne in a grotesque toast to betrayal. Delia's eyes narrowed, registering the scene with cold detachment. Jennifer's motives were clear, her ruthlessness undisguised. Delia checked Blume's pockets and found a set of car keys. She was unaware of where Jennifer was going, so she followed her.

Delia pressed ahead with silent efficiency, her path a direct line to the exit. Her thoughts spiraled, calculating the repercussions of Jennifer's actions. With Blume dead, the plan had shifted again. Delia needed to stay ahead, needed to anticipate the next move.

She reached the door and called for the elevator. She had to hurry if she was going to catch Jennifer. The door opened, and she tapped the button marked with a G. She assumed Jennifer had a car here, since she didn't take Blume's keys.

The elevator opened, and she pulled back as Jennifer slipped into a dark gray Mercedes, pulled out of the space and sped to the exit. Since she knew Jennifer had no idea what she looked like, she stepped out and pushed the button on the key fob. A blue Mercedes in the space next to the one Jennifer just left beeped, and she hit the button, slid in and followed Jennifer.

Delia followed at a distance, keeping the Mercedes in view as much as she could. She slowed as the car turned onto a little-used road, passed through a broken gate and drove onto the crumbling tarmac towards the far end of the field.

Delia drove past the abandoned airport until she found a spot nearer the end of the runway where she could park the Mercedes unseen. She grabbed her backpack and slid out, leaving the door ajar. She crawled under a cut piece of the chain-link fence and, staying low, raced towards the end of the runway.

Fifty yards from Jennifer's Mercedes and out of sight behind a small berm, she crawled to the edge and pulled her binoculars out of her backpack. She settled in and scanned the area. The sun was moving closer to the small hills, and she waited.

Delia spotted Blume's soldiers in various spots around the runway, hidden from all except for those with tactical awareness. She mentally marked their locations. She was going to need to lower the odds if she was going to be successful.

She left her backpack behind the berm and made her way down the runway until she was out of sight of the first soldier she marked. She ran across the crumbling tarmac and entered the field. She moved slowly, creeping like a leopard on the hunt. She found the first guard sighting through his rifle scope. She approached him, and before he could react, her knife sliced through his windpipe, and he gurgled as his life drained into the dirt. One down, God knew how many left.

She moved to the next one. By the time she saw the approaching SUVs, she had taken out four of Blume's men. She hoped it would be enough to even the odds. She raced back to her backpack and raised her binoculars.

The SUVs stopped next to Jennifer's Mercedes. Several men exited, forming a perimeter that warned but didn't threaten. Delia viewed the ballet of ruthlessness, each movement choreographed with care. A giant emerged, cigarette smoke trailing and disappearing in the breeze. Then came Tommy, small and afraid, with a cover over his head, his hands tied in front of him. She couldn't look away. Not even as the second ghost emerged from another car: Morrison.

His head was down, but Delia had seen the black-and-blue spots before he lowered it. They led him to the front of the vehicles. His hands were tied behind his back, and his legs were hobbled. He looked like the past few hours had not been kind to him. The guard positioned him next to the lead vehicle, and they waited. He looked up, spotted Tommy and tried to move. The rifle butt slammed into his stomach, and he collapsed. The guard left him there, and he looked up. His eyes filled with tears.

A second set of vehicles appeared on the runway and headed in their direction. They parked opposite the first set of SUVs, and a group of hard men and women slid out of the vehicles and formed a protective barrier.

Delia's pulse quickened as she tracked the scene, her exterior calm but her mind racing ahead. The team formed a line of protection, their weapons slung but ready. They moved like wolves, hungry and aware, surrounding the convoy in a display of strength. Fifty yards separated Delia from them, a distance both vast and intimate in the fading light. She knew every eye was on Jennifer, every gaze measuring her intentions.

David slid out of the lead vehicle and stepped towards her. Jennifer stepped from behind Blume's men and approached him. They met in the middle and shook hands. Delia couldn't hear what was being said, but she imagined it went something like, "Where is Blume, and who are you?" and her answer would be, "Blume is dead, and this has always been my operation."

David shook his head and moved back a step, creating some distance between himself and Jennifer.

Morrison looked up and spotted Jennifer, and his look told Delia everything she needed to know. He had no idea his wife was part of the deal. He tried to speak out and was hit again with the rifle and slumped to his knees. Jennifer walked over, pushed the guard aside and kneeled next to him. She held his face with her hand and spoke to him, then pushed his chin aside and stood.

The stillness grew heavy, anticipation a thick haze that hung in the atmosphere. Delia stood firm, her heart a steady drumbeat against the pressure of what was to come. The scene unfolded with a slow and deliberate tension, a waiting game where even the slightest twitch could signal the start of something catastrophic.

The boy's appearance sent a ripple through her, an emotional tremor that she couldn't suppress. Tommy looked smaller than she remembered, the time and distance casting him in a new and vulnerable light. The grip on his arm was tight, a possessive claim that sent a surge of anger and purpose through Delia.

Morrison tried to stand, but his legs wouldn't hold him, so he stayed as he was and stared at Tommy. His expression told Delia that he had given up and believed that he and the boy were going to die. She was outnumbered already. She waited for the last group to arrive. The Iranians were the key to all of this, and she thought about how Jennifer was going to explain the lack of plans. She held her spot and waited. She didn't have to wait long.

A third small procession of cars entered the area and parked. The doors opened, and several Iranian soldiers exited the vehicles and positioned themselves ahead of the cars. From

Delia's position, Jennifer's group held a tactical advantage, since much of her contingent was hidden. If the shooting started, many people were going to die. She had to get to Tommy in time.

Jennifer approached the Iranian negotiator. She held out her hand, and he looked at her. He reached out and took her hand. He was a tall, dapper-looking man with a trimmed beard and wearing an expensive suit. His mocha complexion was flawless, but his black eyes were piercing. Jennifer hesitated, then shook the proffered hand.

Jennifer spoke first, her voice cutting through the hush. "I'm the one you'll be negotiating with."

Her words struck with the precision of a guided missile. The negotiator's mouth curved into a thin smile, amused and calculating.

"Very well," he said, his voice filled with authority. "You say you have what I want. Then show me." He never questioned where Blume was.

Jennifer raised her hand, revealing a slim USB drive glinting in the setting sunlight.

"Inside this drive are the blueprints for your next-generation fighter," she said, letting her claim settle between them.

The negotiator glanced at his entourage, then nodded. In the blink of an eye, his aide approached with an open laptop, its black screen reflecting the tension in the air.

The aide held the laptop in the palm of one hand and plugged in the drive. Fingers hovered over the keyboard as the machine booted up, the hard drive's whir a drumbeat of anticipation. Jennifer held her breath, watching the screen flicker to life.

But nothing appeared. No folders, no files. Just an empty directory blinking back at them. The silence that followed was worse than a barrage of gunfire. The negotiator's eyes narrowed.

"Is this some kind of joke?" His words dropped like a hammer. His English was perfect.

Jennifer stood unmoved, staring at the man with the laptop. Her heart pounded, but her voice remained steady. "Check again."

The aide's fingers danced across the keys, but every attempt produced the same blank display.

A trace of anger passed over the negotiator's face. Jennifer saw the veneer of diplomacy crack, revealing something harder, colder. He straightened, voice low and dangerous.

"This drive is empty." The accusation was rhetorical; he already knew.

Jennifer didn't flinch. She let that moment hang, then met his glare head-on.

"Empty. How is that possible?" she repeated, each syllable a challenge. "Or did your man transfer the files without us knowing?" Her jaw set as she leaned towards the hidden holster at her side.

The negotiator stared at her. "What are you accusing us of?" The tension coiled tighter with each passing second. The sun cast long shadows behind Jennifer—shadows shaped like soldiers, weapons, resolute defiance.

In that electric instant, Jennifer's purpose crystallized. She wasn't here to trade designs; she was here to fracture his plans and steal his money. The realization registered on the negotiator's face: she had orchestrated this standoff and now held the upper hand.

He drew himself to his full height. "You've wasted my time," he said, voice cold as steel. His words carried the promise of retribution.

Jennifer detected the coil of danger in the air—guns in holsters, troops poised at the edges of the tarmac, an entire regime's honor on the line. Yet she never wavered. One hand rested against the grip of her concealed weapon, her heartbeat echoing in her palm.

David stepped next to Jennifer. "Is there a problem?" he asked.

The negotiator stared at him. "Yes, there is a problem. Your partner here is trying to cheat us. There is no file."

David stared at Jennifer. "What the fuck is going on? We had a deal. Where is the file?"

Her gaze never left the negotiator. Every muscle in her body spoke of readiness. "I'm here," she thought. "I won't be browbeaten. I will end this on my terms."

The final moment approached, a taut crescendo of silence and promise. Jennifer had delivered her message. Now it was time for the real negotiations to begin.

Showdown at Dawn

The shot cracked like a starter pistol. Jennifer's bullet hit the Iranian negotiator in the chest, and he flew backward, the bullet's echo fading into rapid, lethal percussion. She dove and tackled the young man with the laptop and forced him down. Her breath came hard, matching the roar of gunfire that erupted across the airstrip.

Delia raced across the field, covering fifty yards in a flash. She fired as she ran, her shots accurate and deadly. Two men dropped, unaware of their fall. Jennifer's voice was a spear, directing Blume's men to protect her and the laptop. The dust stung her eyes as gunfire thundered off the cracked tarmac.

She ran towards the cars, looking for some protection from all the bullets piercing the air. She glanced out of the corner of her eye as David was hit while he was pulling a pistol from inside his coat. He never got off a shot before he hit the ground, blood blossoming on his shirt. She wanted to stop, but her goal lay elsewhere.

She shot the big guy holding Tommy, and he fell to the ground. The second shot to his head ended his role in the fight. She grabbed Tommy and pulled him behind an SUV. She pushed him down as bullets peppered the SUV. Delia poked up her head and fired in response, dropping her magazine and reloading.

She looked across the tarmac and spotted Morrison lying on his side, his legs pulled up to his chest. She couldn't tell if he was alive or dead, but it was time to get Tommy out of the fight. She removed the hood and looked him in the eye. His small body shook, and he had tears in his eyes. She pulled a knife from her pocket and cut the bands around his hands.

"Your dad sent me to get you away from here," she said.

"Is my dad here?" he asked, his voice cracking.

"I don't know, but we need to get out of here."

Tommy nodded, and Delia rose just as a guy came around the SUV. She snapped off a shot, and he went down in a lump. Delia took Tommy's hand and led him towards the field. Gunfire roared all around them.

She fired as she moved, each shot a timed counterpoint to their aggression. The gunpowder clung to the air as she slipped past the SUVs, looking for an escape route, her senses alive. Delia tracked the movement of Blume's men, their efforts to flank the shooters from the Iranian and Organization contingents, a dance she knew all too well. Her throat was tight, the dust coating it; they ducked behind another vehicle, her weapon steady and her mind clear.

Delia's tactical training kicked in, every instinct a honed response to the chaos. Her shots were measured; she conserved ammunition with the discipline of knowing how quickly it could run out. She could hear Jennifer's voice yelling orders, feeling the urgency as Blume's men pushed harder to protect her.

The airstrip was a battlefield, but Delia advanced with certainty, every decision calculated. The fading light cast long shadows, transforming the terrain into an advantage she refused to squander. She saw a gap, a momentary lapse in the net closing around the runway. Delia bolted for it, her feet pounding against the cracked asphalt, Tommy following at her heels. She pushed Tommy behind the SUV.

Delia kneeled beside him, his small form huddled and trembling on the tarmac. The boy's clothes were dirty and torn, his face streaked with tears and dust. Blood spatter marked the concrete nearby.

Tommy flinched at every sound, his eyes wide with shock. Delia spoke to him in soft, measured tones, checking him for injuries while maintaining a protective stance between him and the carnage.

"I will keep you safe," she told him, her voice steady despite her own exhaustion. "No one's going to hurt you anymore."

Tommy's response was a silent nod, the movement almost imperceptible. His gaze darted around the airstrip, taking in the aftermath of violence and betrayal. The Turkish landscape stretched beyond, vast and indifferent. The late afternoon chill clung to the air, but Delia stayed close to him, absorbing the fear that radiated from his small body.

Her own breath came hard, each inhale indicative of the desperate struggle. She felt the fatigue in her limbs, but she wouldn't let it show, wouldn't let Tommy see any hint of vulnerability. He needed her strength, her assurance that the nightmare was over.

The echoes of gunfire still seemed to ring in the distance, the phantom sounds keeping Tommy's nerves taut and ready to snap. Delia shifted, positioning herself so that he wouldn't have to look at the blood or the bodies, at the reminders of how close he'd come to losing everything. She repeated her promise, letting each word sink in.

"You're safe," she said again. "I won't let anyone hurt you."

The last rays of sunlight sat over the horizon, turning the landscape gold and the shadows long. They both flinched as a distant engine roared to life, a reminder that the danger might not be as distant as she claimed. But Delia held her ground, kept her focus on the boy who needed her more than ever. She would protect him. It was all she could do.

Delia felt the pressure of the battle settle on her shoulders, as real as the dust that covered them both. But she pushed it aside, locked it away with the same ruthless efficiency she'd used to lock away so many other things. All that mattered was Tommy, his safety, his belief that this time, she was telling the truth.

He looked at her, a question in his eyes, a need so raw it undid her. But Delia stayed firm, her exhaustion hidden behind the mask of certainty she'd worn for years.

"No one's going to hurt you," she said one final time, her voice a lifeline in the stillness.

Tommy leaned into her, the trust in the gesture more profound than words. Delia felt it, absorbed it and let herself believe it was true.

The bullets kept coming, but she kept moving. The dust choked the air. Men and women lay dead and dying. She pushed Tommy into the SUV.

"Stay here and keep your head down," she said.

She closed the door and rejoined the fight. Her goal was to reach Morrison and David. She fired from behind cover, diving low and rising with relentless speed. Delia's boldness was as sure as her aim, each bullet a silent promise of survival. Sirens sounded, and she saw flashing lights at the far end of the runway.

She could feel the momentum shift, a subtle but undeniable change in the pressure. Her advantage was slight but real. She seized it, pushing harder as she slipped between vehicles. Her body ached with effort, but she didn't let it slow her. She wouldn't stop.

The gunfire was a drumbeat, a percussive rhythm that scored the entire scene. Delia was part of it but separate. She had to be. Each shot, each movement was vital and deliberate. She sidestepped the gunfire like water through a sieve, elusive and impossible to contain.

Amid the fight, Delia spotted Jennifer and Blume's soldier making their way to an SUV. She carried the laptop in her hand. Delia looked over to where she had first seen her and saw the young Iranian man lying on the ground with a bullet hole in his head.

They reached the SUV and opened the doors, the soldier taking the driver's seat. They slid inside, and the SUV roared ahead, running down an Iranian soldier. The sound was horrible, and Delia fired into the back window of the escaping SUV. The window shattered, but the SUV kept going, bouncing across the field, heading towards the broken fence.

The gunfire was subsiding. Delia fired into the chaos behind her as she broke into a sprint. She ran towards Morrison and kneeled beside him, her senses on high alert. She rolled him flat and saw the bullet hole in his shoulder, but it was the one in his thigh that worried her. It was bleeding a lot. She unbuckled his belt, slid it from his pants, wrapped it around his thigh and pulled it tight. He winced as she made it fast. His eyes opened.

"Tommy?" he asked.

Delia smiled. "I have him." His eyes closed, and his head slumped. Delia checked his pulse and turned. David lay fifteen feet away, and she raced to his side. Bullets followed her like angry hornets, each one a sting she refused to let hit. Her feet pounded the ground, every step a defiance of the danger.

Delia reached David and pulled him behind an SUV. She shot an approaching Iranian soldier and laid David flat on the ground. His pulse was weak, and he had lost a lot of blood. She touched his face, and a tear rolled down her cheek. David looked up, and his face lit up like he was looking at an angel.

"Delia, are you here? Are you real?"

Before she could answer, his eyes closed, and his breathing became shallow. Delia stood and took in the scene. The gunfire had stopped, and she spotted the emergency vehicles nearing. She had to get clear of the scene and then find Jennifer.

She ran to the SUV where she'd left Tommy, opened the door and grabbed Tommy by the arm. He climbed out, and they ran across the field towards the fence. They slid under the fence and ran to the Mercedes. They climbed in, and Delia started the engine and headed towards the city.

Delia pulled out her phone and dialed a number. The phone rang, and the call connected. "I need another safe house," she said.

"Give me ten minutes," said Hamza. "I will text you an address. Are you okay? I heard about a firefight at the old airport."

"I'm fine," she said as she looked at the blood dripping from her shoulder. The bullet had hit like a sledgehammer and had knocked her against the hood of an SUV. She had staggered behind the vehicle and returned fire. The pain burned in her mind.

She reached into a pocket in her backpack, pulled out a tampon and pushed it into the hole. She winced and gritted her teeth as she sealed the wound, and her vision blurred. She shook her head to clear the cobwebs. She had too much to do to worry about it now.

"I need another favor. Morrison is at the airport. He's hurt bad, and . . ." She hesitated for a few seconds. "My husband was also shot. He lost a significant amount of blood."

The silence on the phone was deafening. "David is here in Istanbul. Did he know you were here?" asked Hamza.

"I don't know. He's working for the Organization."

"Since when?" asked Hamza.

"I have no idea. I guess I wasn't the only one in the marriage with secrets."

"What are you going to do?" he asked.

"Right now, I need Tommy someplace safe. Then I'll figure it out."

Delia disconnected the call and dialed another number. Harper answered.

"Oh, thank god," he said. "The word is out about a huge firefight at an old, abandoned airport. The authorities are reporting many dead and injured. I was worried you might be in the middle."

Delia laughed. "I was. I have Tommy. We're heading to a safe house. Morrison and David are injured badly. I had to leave them."

"What about Blume?" he asked.

"Blume is dead. Jennifer Morrison killed him at his apartment. She grabbed a laptop from the Iranians. She plans to transfer the funds for the buy into her account and disappear. I need you to work the city cameras from the old airport and see where she's going. She's in an SUV with a shattered rear window."

"That's easier said than done. There's not that much CCTV coverage in that part of the city. Let me see if I've got any satellites I can tap into. It will take a bit, but I'll do what I can. Are you going after her?"

"Yes. She masterminded this whole thing, and she put Tommy in danger."

"But your job is done. You saved Tommy, and we prevented the Iranians from getting the fighter plans. You should head for the airport and get the hell out of here."

"Not yet," she said. "I have this one thing left to take care of."

Harper agreed to track Jennifer down and let Delia know when he found her, and she disconnected the call. Her phone chimed with a text. She read the address and put the phone on the center console. Once she got Tommy settled, she would make sure Jennifer Morrison paid for all the damage she'd caused.

Delia parked the Mercedes on the street and led Tommy to the address Hamza had texted. They climbed two flights of stairs, and Delia entered the code Hamza gave her and opened the door. They stepped through the door, and Delia pulled her pistol and pointed it at the shadow that emerged from what turned out to be the kitchen. The woman raised her hands.

"I have been sent to help you," she said, her English near perfect. Delia lowered the pistol.

"Who are you?" asked Delia.

The woman was heavyset with long gray hair and wore a flower-print dress. She smiled at Delia.

"Names are not important," she said.

Delia looked at the interior of the safe house. This one looked like someone's apartment. It was clean and well-furnished, with modern furniture and décor. The walls were painted bright white, making the space feel airy and clean. Delia's eyes scanned over the furniture, noticing the well-kept couches and tables, and the lack of clutter or mess.

The air inside the safe house was fresh, devoid of any musty scents. Delia could detect hints of lavender and vanilla, perhaps from candles or air fresheners carefully placed around the room.

The woman walked over and looked at Tommy. "Let's get you settled, young man."

She walked him to a worn couch and helped him sit. She walked back to Delia.

"I have food cooking on the stove." She spotted the blood on Delia's shirt. "Go take a shower, and when you are finished, I will clean and dress your wound."

Delia dropped her go bag, grabbed clean pants and a shirt from it and walked into the bathroom. A few minutes later, she returned to the main room wearing clean clothes and drying her hair in a towel.

Tommy's sobs slowed as the woman soothed him with gentle words and a soft blanket. Tommy slipped off to sleep, and the woman walked over next to Delia and asked her to follow her. They exited the room, and Delia sat on a kitchen chair. The caretaker cleaned and stitched the holes in Delia's shoulder with the efficiency of a surgeon. Each careful stitch erased the last frayed edge of adrenaline from her nerves. The bullet had passed through and had caused little damage.

Delia ate two helpings of an incredible stew and followed it up with a can of Coke. She set the bowl aside and grabbed her bag. She reloaded four magazines; each click of a fresh bullet being inserted restored a measure of control.

Wrapped in a dark tactical jacket, Delia sat by the window, phone at the ready. She waited for Harper's call confirming Jennifer Morrison's location. While she monitored the safe house's perimeter, Tommy's breathing deepened in the next room.

At last, her phone buzzed. "I've got her. I'm sending her location to your phone," Harper said, voice low but urgent.

Delia nodded to herself, steeling her nerves. She stood, checked her gear one last time and walked towards Tommy's door.

Through the open door, she saw him curled under a wool blanket, his face streaked with dried tears. The caretaker straightened the blanket and offered Delia a small nod of assurance.

Delia drew a steady breath, whispered, "Thank you," and stepped out into the night, ready to finish what she'd started.

The Price of Victory

Jennifer Morrison crouched low in the passenger seat beside one of Blume's men, the SUV barreling across the dusty field, the engine's roar masking the distant gunfire. She dropped the magazine from her pistol and slammed home a full one, chambering a fresh round, eyes scanning the horizon for any stragglers.

Without warning, the rear window erupted inward in a spiderweb of glass. Jennifer yanked her head back as a bullet slammed into the dashboard, inches from where her head had been moments before. The driver's shoulders jerked, and his head slumped. A geyser of blood and brain coated the windshield. The SUV veered, smashing through the old perimeter chain-link fence.

Metal screeched as the vehicle fishtailed sideways, crossed the road and slammed into a lone light pole. Sparks flew. The engine sputtered and died, leaving the thud of Jennifer's heartbeat in her ears.

She yanked off her seatbelt and threw open her door. The evening air was bitter, laced with dust and gunpowder. Sprinting around the crumpled hood, she kneeled and yanked at the limp form draped over the steering wheel. With a grunt, she hauled him free and dropped him onto the cracked concrete.

Jennifer dove into the driver's seat, pushed the starter and prayed the SUV would start. The engine caught, sputtering to life. She eased the SUV off the pole, crunching over debris, and drove down the deserted road leading from the battlefield.

She'd made it. She gazed at the laptop sitting on the seat next to her. All she had to do was keep the program from closing and she could transfer the funds to her various accounts. She had to find a place to pull over, but first she needed to get clear of the old airport.

She tightened her grip on the wheel, every muscle vibrating with adrenaline. The horizon spread before her, empty and unforgiving—but she was moving, escaping the carnage Blume had wrought. As long as she kept driving, she'd stay one step ahead of anyone foolish enough to follow her.

Jennifer's headlights revealed an abandoned gas station, and she pulled into the cracked parking lot and drove behind the building. She stopped and picked up the laptop. Her efforts to keep the program open had paid off.

Jennifer hunched over the battered laptop. The cracked plastic beneath her fingers was sticky with the blood and sweat of this hellish night, but she ignored it, tunneled into her task like a miner after the last vein of gold. The old gas station office stank of mold and diesel, broken blinds lacing the windows with pale stripes of dusk, but all she saw was the glow of the screen, and the columns of numbers blinking back at her. Her first move: rip through the tangle of open windows and processes left by the Iranian coder.

She found the program the Iranians tried to use to transfer the funds, home-brewed but elegant. She admired its sheer paranoia: two-factor authentication, kinetic handshake, even a fail-safe that would shut down the device if it detected the wrong movement.

She hesitated before the final step, then she deleted Blume's account numbers from the transfer protocol and, with a single line of code, injected her own. She hit execute.

The screen froze, a spinning cursor blinking like an accusation. Jennifer gritted her teeth, willed the code to work. If this didn't go through, there was no plan B, no payout, just a cell in some basement and a slow, bloody death. The cursor staggered, then the app flickered, and the money in the Iranian account disappeared. Vanished like it had never existed. She checked the logs: clean as a whistle.

She didn't smile, not yet. There were always shadows in the code, ghosts that could come back to haunt you. She opened her phone, thumbed in her own banking app—a dummy made to look like a dating site, disguised behind layers of plausible deniability—and checked all her aliases.

The first, a charity in Macao, pulsed with seven digits. The next, a Belize shell in the name of a dead tennis pro, updated in real time, the numbers rolling up like a slot machine. Her own personal account, the one she guarded with a kind of superstition, was flush with more money than she'd ever seen outside of a fever dream.

She ran a final security sweep. The program had been brilliant but arrogant, with several hardwired callbacks to Tehran. She scrubbed each one, then ran her own parasite script to make sure the Iranian cyber team would be chasing ghosts for months. Maximum confusion, minimum risk.

She shut down the laptop and tossed it out the window into the weeds behind the gas station. It landed with a satisfying crunch, right in the middle of an oil-stained puddle.

The old her would've felt sad at killing good hardware, but the new her felt nothing.

She started the still-ticking SUV, which somehow hadn't bled out yet, and pointed it towards the city lights. She felt the first wave of exhaustion rolling over her like a summer storm, but she forced her hands to stay steady. There would be time to crash later—if there was a later.

Jennifer saw the lights of Istanbul approach, her thoughts already shifting to what waited at the airport. Her foot pressed the accelerator, chasing the city until the horizon bled to gray. There were still people who wanted her dead, and plenty more who didn't even know her name, but she had won for now. She let herself savor a single, bitter laugh, and then she was gone, the night swallowing the SUV whole as it arrowed towards the future.

***

Unmarked vehicles poured onto the airstrip. Men in dark clothing fanned out, their movements precise as they secured the scene. Morrison, lying unconscious on a stretcher, was lifted into a waiting ambulance. David was stabilized at the scene, IV fluids administered, and he was placed on a stretcher and put in a different ambulance.

Within minutes, silent hands stripped assault rifles, sidearms and shell casings from the bloodied turf. Each bullet was bagged, cataloged and photographed under the harsh glare of portable floodlights. Nothing left to chance, not a single clue overlooked.

The police commander glared as he approached Hamza's team leader.

"Who the fuck do you think you are? This is my crime scene. You have no right." His displeasure was palpable, and his voice thundered with the threat of lodging a formal complaint. "I want your name and the name of your boss."

His fury simmered just beneath the surface, like a volcano ready to erupt. He wasn't used to being pushed aside by others. The team leader looked at him and pulled his phone from his pocket. Ignoring the fire in the police commander's eyes, he dialed a number and spoke briefly. He acknowledged and handed the phone to the police commander.

"Who the fuck is this?" he shouted into the phone.

The color drained from his face, and he stood straighter. His ire was swiftly extinguished.

"Yes, sir. I have many units that do not have computers in their vehicles." He listened. "Yes, sir. Computers would be most appreciated." He listened again. "Yes, sir. I'll have my officers clear the site immediately. Thank you, sir."

He handed the phone back to the team leader and scratched his head. He turned from the team leader, walked to the tarmac and ordered all his officers to stop what they were doing and leave the site. There was some grumbling, but they all complied.

Bodies of the dead and wounded were gathered with trained efficiency. Black-suited men carried them away on tarps, stacking them on the tarmac, waiting for the trucks that would make the bodies disappear. Those who were still breathing were shot. Pools of blood were mopped up and rinsed with chemical agents. The stench of death and gunpowder faded, replaced by the bitterness of bleach.

The echo of violence was muted, replaced by a clinical orderliness that left the field empty except for the battered earth and the creak of evidence carts. Those vehicles still drivable disappeared into the night. The others were placed on trailers and hauled away. By the time the first light of dawn split the sky, not a single trace of the firefight remained, except for the memories of those who had died and the silent, implacable purpose of the men who had cleaned it all away.

Hamza's black government SUV coasted to a stop behind the military jeep on the cracked tarmac of the abandoned airstrip. The Turkish general, his immaculately pressed tunic adorned with medals glinting in the morning sun, stood with his back to them, a smoldering cigar poised between his fingers as he surveyed the tarmac and field. The bleach was still heavy in the air.

Hamza slipped from the back seat and approached, fastening his jacket with precise movements. He stopped next to the general, and they shook hands.

"By the time police units arrived," said Hamza, "the firefight was over. They were arresting the survivors when my team arrived, and we took over the site under your authority. The police commander was not pleased and threatened to lodge a formal complaint. He was placated when we informed him that several of his units would receive new computers. We identified Iranians, locals and several Americans and Europeans. Blume's body was not among the victims. My sources tell me that a man matching his description was found in an alley near the Iranian embassy with a bullet wound in his head. His penthouse is being scrubbed as we speak."

The general puffed on his cigar, ash drifting to the cracked concrete below. He looked at Hamza.

"Any survivors of this . . . battle?" asked the general. "And what happened to the ones the police were arresting?"

Hamza smiled. "There were no survivors, General."

The general puffed his cigar. "That's good, Hamza. Very good." He scanned the area. "Your men did an excellent job cleaning up the area. There is barely a blade of grass out of place."

Hamza nodded. He didn't think it was prudent to tell the general that two American operatives were in the hospital undergoing surgery. That was a secret he would keep to himself.

The general ground the cigar into the jeep's tire tread, smoke trailing upward. "How the hell were we not aware this business was taking place right under our noses?" Suspicion flickered behind his cold eyes. "We have been negotiating with Iran for weeks. How were we not aware of their subterfuge?"

Hamza turned and faced the general. "We were played by all parties involved. Blume was representing everyone and played them all for fools. The Americans had no idea that they had a mole in the embassy who was about to steal a major secret, and somehow the Organization got involved, because there was money to be made."

"Did Iran get the plans for the American stealth fighter? And what became of the American who was fingered as the mole?" asked the general.

Hamza composed his thoughts. "The Iranians did not receive them. My understanding is that those plans have been moved and are not accessible. As far as Morrison, the American we believed was behind the plan to steal the documents, he has been cleared. It turned out he was set up by his wife, who also worked in the embassy, and he was forced to play a role after his young son was kidnapped. He was killed during the battle, along with the representative from the Organization."

"Set up by his wife," said the general. "That's cold. Do we have her in custody?"

Hamza smiled. "I have it on good authority that she will not leave the country."

The general turned and stared down the runway. "Blume's death will send ripples through many countries. He had his fingers in a lot of pies. People will demand answers."

"It's a shame that he found himself in a bad neighborhood and was mugged and killed," said Hamza.

The general laughed. "Yes, it is truly a shame. We must do something about the lawlessness in our city."

The general climbed into the passenger seat of his jeep, and his driver raced over and slid onto his seat. He started the engine. The general looked at Hamza and laughed. The jeep pulled away, and Hamza stood next to his SUV.

Delia eased open the SUV door, slid out and stood beside Hamza, dust kicking up around her boots. Hamza's gaze was steady, no surprise in his eyes, the faint curve of relief in his smile.

"The general looked pleased," she said.

Hamza folded his arms against the late morning warmth. "He did because he thinks we've tied up every loose end." He paused, then offered a tight smile. "I kept quiet about David and Morrison."

Her shoulders relaxed. "Thank you," she said, sincerity sharpening each word. She measured the distance between them, secrets hanging in the air.

"Now," said Hamza, "we need a plan for Jennifer Morrison and the Organization."

Delia tilted her head. "From what we could find, Jennifer Morrison is on her own. With Blume's network destroyed, she has no one to turn to. She is working to secure documents to leave the country. I have eyes on her, and I will deal with her. As far as the Organization is concerned, if you go after them, there will be repercussions. You leave them to me."

His nod was curt but approving. "All right. Will you need support—satellite feeds, safe houses?"

"I've got contacts," said Delia. "We've already accessed three of her accounts, and we're holding the funds in a reserve account. Once we finish, those funds will be given to you. You can use the funds to work something out with the Iranians. They might be more receptive to your negotiations. Once my work here is done, you'll not see me again. Thank you for all your help."

Hamza exhaled, tension slipping from his stance. "Understood. The general will use this information and make it hard for them to say no to anything. He is also grateful that they do not have the fighter plans. That will be a big tool in his toolbox."

They walked to the SUV and slid in, and the driver pulled away. It had been a long night, and Delia still had work to do.

Debriefing and Doubts

The young operative sat rigidly in a polished conference room at the Organization's safe house in Ankara, the sounds of the city muffled out through thick windows. He had slept little since he was spirited out of Istanbul. He delivered the mission debrief to the director and two silent analysts who took notes in the background.

The room was sterile and formal, with shadows formed by the lights breaking the monotony. He recounted the operation: Jennifer Morrison's elaborate betrayal, the airstrip confrontation, Blume's death by her hand and Tommy's rescue. His voice remained professional and detached, but his fingers tightened around the water glass when describing the child's terror. The director observed him with paternal scrutiny, noting how he omitted mention of his injuries. The rain pattered against the windows.

"The airstrip was compromised," he said, his words crisp and unwavering. "Blume's men attempted an ambush. Everyone returned fire. It was a double cross."

His eyes flickered towards the director, gauging his reaction. He remained impassive, a figure of calculated authority. The operative continued, unperturbed by the director's lack of visible response.

"Morrison's son was being used as leverage," he explained, the mention of the boy a crack in his otherwise flawless delivery. "Rumors around the embassy are that Jennifer Morrison was the mole, and she set the whole thing up, including trying to frame her husband."

One analyst shifted, the sound loud in the quiet space, but neither interrupted nor questioned his account. His focus remained on the director, his body a study in controlled tension. The room felt close, the walls pressing in.

"Morrison and Blume?" The director's voice was low, each syllable precise.

The young man didn't hesitate, though the inquiry brought a tightness to his jaw. "Morrison was spirited away by Turkish Intelligence. His wounds were significant. We have been unable to locate him. We received a report that Blume's body was found in a bad part of Istanbul and that he had been mugged and killed."

"What about the wife?" asked the director.

The young man fidgeted. "We have been unable to locate her as well."

The director frowned. "That's not good. With Blume gone, we can deny our involvement in this whole sordid affair, but if Jennifer Morrison is still alive, there could be repercussions."

The rain on the windows increased, the light drizzle turning into a steady rhythm. The young man took a breath, the pause more telling than any slip of composure. He knew how the story ended; he just didn't know how the director would read it.

He delivered the rest of his report with mechanical precision, the professional distance in his tone at odds with the memories he recounted. He described Jennifer Morrison's plan, her callous willingness to sacrifice her stepson for freedom and leverage.

"Her diplomatic connections may complicate the situation," he conceded, his voice a brittle monotone that revealed more than he'd intended.

The director listened without interruption, his attention to the man's words unwavering. The man felt his scrutiny, the sharpness of it cutting through his measured detachment.

He avoided his gaze, looking instead at the glass of water in front of him. His fingers curled around it.

His voice caught, an imperceptible crack that the director seemed to notice. The director leaned back in his chair, watching him with a mixture of curiosity and something else—something that might have been concern.

The rain grew louder, filling the room with its steady, insistent presence. He finished his report, his words trailing into silence as the tension thickened. The room seemed to close in around him, the storm's intensity a reminder of all he tried to suppress.

The director remained silent, his expression thoughtful. He let the pause linger, a tactical use of time that forced the young man to sit with his own uneasiness. He held his ground, refusing to show the exhaustion that threatened to crack his composure.

The analysts continued to take notes, their pens scratching across paper. His injuries ached beneath the surface, a reminder of all he'd endured and all he'd omitted from his account.

When the director spoke, his voice was a low, measured rumble. "What happened to David?" he asked, the question laden with implications he chose not to acknowledge.

"The last I saw David," he said, "he was lying on the ground in a puddle of blood."

The director gazed at him. "And you just left him there?"

The young man squirmed in the hard chair. "I had no choice. People were dying all around us."

"Yet you survived, when so many others did not. Why is that?" asked the director, his eyes burning holes through the man's head.

He couldn't answer. His body shook in the chair.

The director inclined his head, a gesture that could have been approval or dismissal. The young man couldn't tell which. The anxiety gnawed at him, but he maintained his professional veneer.

As the rain hammered the windows, he knew that his report had ended, but he had no idea what lay ahead.

The director rose from his chair after the young man's report and walked to the window, where rain streamed down the glass. He offered measured praise for his success, his voice carrying the force of authority as he straightened his already perfect tie.

"The boy is safe and no longer under our control. The fighter plans have disappeared. David is missing and possibly dead, and your report made it sound like this was a success." He paused, then delivered the warning about diplomatic complications and political fallout. "Turkey is demanding explanations. My contact at the State Department is scrambling. Blume has powerful friends who don't appreciate being embarrassed."

His reflection in the window showed a concern that his words didn't convey. The young man responded with a curt nod, already gathering his things, his movements betraying exhaustion despite his composed face. The director scrutinized him with an unreadable expression before dismissing the analysts with a subtle gesture, leaving them momentarily alone.

The analysts slipped out, their departure as quiet and efficient as their presence had been. The young man grabbed the strap of his backpack, a moment of tension that spoke to his internal state. He refused to let fatigue overtake him, though it pressed down with relentless force.

The director turned but remained by the window, his posture relaxed but his gaze intense. "Your report was thorough," he said, his tone neutral. "But you never said how you escaped or detailed your injuries."

He met the director's eyes, his own expression neutral. "They were minor," he replied, the dismissal more revealing than any admission. "Nothing that compromised the mission."

The director turned and faced the rain-streaked glass again, his reflection a ghostly figure that seemed to scrutinize the young man more than his direct gaze.

"Complications are inevitable," he said, almost to himself. "But you've handled worse."

His confidence was unspoken but clear, a vote of trust that left the young man both reassured and wary. He sensed the layers of his approval, the strategic calculation that lay beneath every word.

"You'll want me to lie low for a while," the young man said, the statement not quite a question. His voice was firm, but the edges frayed, his exhaustion seeping through the cracks.

The director nodded, the gesture slow and considered. "Just until the dust settles," he confirmed, his voice a study in composed authority. "The situation will stabilize, and then we'll see where your talents are most needed."

The young man absorbed his words, the implications both clear and unsettling. He couldn't shake the feeling that he was a piece on a chessboard, his every move expected and controlled.

His breath came shallow, a sign of the internal pressure he fought to contain. He understood the game they were playing, but he couldn't escape the suspicion that the rules had changed.

"You did well," the director finished, the compliment both simple and complex.

The young man smiled. He walked out, the door closing behind him, leaving the tension and the rain to fill the space he left behind.

The director nodded to the two men in suits standing in the shadows. They acknowledged and left by another door.

***

Harper's satellite dump was a revelation that mapped Jennifer Morrison's escape with merciless clarity. From the first pixelated frame, Delia marked Morrison's every movement: an orchestrated route up the Bosphorus, the battered SUV weaving through traffic as if it too were running from something.

By the time Jennifer reached her safe house, a low-slung, unremarkable flat on the city's European side wedged between a kebab shop and a shuttered hotel, Delia already had three approaches and two exits in mind.

Delia slipped into a small cafe, ordered a strong coffee and sat at a table by the window watching the building, waiting like a lioness ready to strike her prey. From across the street, she spotted Jennifer emerge minutes later, her face obscured by dark glasses and a colored scarf. Delia laughed. So much for a subtle disguise.

The walk was brisk but never hurried, the large black duffel slung over her shoulder. A prop designed to look more like gym gear than an escape kit. Delia's first thought was that Jennifer's tradecraft was a joke, but then she noticed the way Morrison's gaze swept the street—a lopsided attempt at surveillance detection—and how she doubled back on herself, ducking into shallow spaces. All the tells of someone who'd seen too many spy movies and who worked for the CIA but had never been out in the field.

Delia exited the cafe, hands deep in the pockets of the black windbreaker she'd bought at a market stall three hours earlier. She let Jennifer gain a block's lead, then shadowed her along the gray-washed avenue. An old man with a cane hobbled by and tipped his hat; Delia smiled automatically, then let the expression fall, her mind already cycling through contingencies. The air was damp, and the sky pressed down, low and threatening.

They wove through a maze of side streets, Morrison attempting more tradecraft maneuvers—a sudden U-turn at a crosswalk, a dive into an arcade, a purposeful linger at a flower stall. Delia saw through each one, recognizing moves copied from TV shows and YouTube tutorials: too obvious, too contrived, telegraphing fear instead of masking it. She kept her distance, adjusting her pace and posture so she vanished into the crowd, just another face in the city's morning shuffle.

But as the route moved eastward, Delia appreciated the subtlety in Jennifer's methods. The hesitations were deliberate, the mistakes rehearsed. At one turn, Jennifer ducked into a laundromat, the door closing behind her, but Delia did not follow. She walked to the end of the block, counting the minutes, then caught sight of Jennifer through the front window, head down, fingers tapping on her phone, the duffel propped at her feet. Delia realized then that Morrison wasn't running. She was waiting for someone.

For the next forty-five minutes, Delia orchestrated her surveillance with surgical patience. She saw Jennifer leave the laundromat, this time with a limp—a calculated affectation, perhaps, but still amateurish in its inconsistency.

She followed Jennifer along a series of small stalls, past rows of glassy-eyed mannequins displaying European and American clothes and piles of cheap citrus. At one stall, Jennifer purchased a SIM card, but the transaction was clumsy, her hands shaking as she fumbled with the packaging.

By the time Jennifer reached the central business district, the wind had picked up, carrying with it the scent of diesel and wet stone as a fine drizzle began. Delia found higher ground at a cafe terrace overlooking the street. She ordered a coffee, then trained her gaze down to the cobblestones below, where Jennifer paced, checking her phone every few seconds. The cafe's owner hovered, but Delia's icy stare dissuaded him from conversation.

Delia watched Jennifer pull out her phone. She typed furiously, then moved off in a new direction, hugging the shadows as she ducked beneath some construction scaffolding and disappeared. Delia was on her feet, moving with the fluidity of someone who'd been doing this longer than she could remember.

She reached the construction site in time to see Jennifer slip through a rusted service door and down into a tunnel of rain-soaked gray concrete—an old maintenance passage that ran parallel to the building.

Delia followed, her shoes silent on the damp concrete. The chill in the tunnel was refreshing, a world apart from the muggy city above. Fifty yards in, she found Jennifer stopped at a fork, heartbeat visible in the tremor of her hands. Delia waited, patient as bedrock, while Jennifer rooted through her duffel, withdrawing a thick manila envelope. Delia's eyes sharpened.

She pulled her phone from her pocket and snapped two quick photos, sending them to Harper with a single-line text: **Target in handoff mode.** She waited for Harper's reply, her eyes never leaving Jennifer. The signal in the tunnel was weak, so it took more time for the message to be transmitted. Delia used the time to study Jennifer's nervous habits, the way her foot tapped out a frantic Morse code against the floor. She almost felt sorry for her.

A series of footsteps echoed behind them, two sets, deliberate and measured. Jennifer heard them too, clutched the envelope closer to her chest. She looked like she intended to run. Delia waited, counting the steps, then watched as Jennifer met two men: one tall and gaunt, the other squat with a wrestler's build. They boxed Jennifer in, voices low and urgent.

Delia read their lips: "You have the money?" Jennifer nodded, hand shaking as she handed over the envelope.

Delia waited. The taller man looked in the envelope and thumbed the contents. He smiled through crooked and missing teeth. The shorter man pulled an envelope out of his ragged coat pocket and handed it to her. They said something Delia couldn't hear, and she noticed Jennifer pull back.

The two men laughed and disappeared down the dark hall. Jennifer stood for a second and worked to control her shaking hands. She opened the envelope and pulled out a passport and other smaller documents. She looked through them, tossed the envelope and put the items in her pocket. She turned and retraced her steps through the abandoned construction site.

Delia moved like lightning, snaking through the site to get ahead of Jennifer. She stood behind a stack of cans of paint and waited, her knife in her hand. A noise echoed farther in the tunnel, and Jennifer turned as she was walking to check behind her. As she turned back, a searing pain sprang from her abdomen, and she stopped short.

The bloodstain spread across the lower part of her tan T-shirt, and she stared in disbelief; the pain was intense, and she leaned against the stack of cans. Her legs gave out, and she slid, knocking over some of the cans with a clatter. Her bag fell off her shoulder and settled on the floor next to her.

A dark shadow moved towards her, and she looked up, her eyes filled with tears. Her mouth opened, but no words came out. Delia kneeled next to her, the bloody knife still in her hand.

"You set up your husband to be the fall guy and you were willing to sacrifice your son, for what, money?" asked Delia.

Jennifer's eyes grew wide, and she tried to squirm away. Delia kept her place.

Jennifer choked back tears; her voice quivered. "Blume and me," she said, but she never finished. "Tommy wasn't my son. James's first marriage. He meant nothing to me." Blood leaked from the corner of her mouth. Her body shook. "Why?" she asked, a spasm moving through her body.

Delia smiled. "I hate people who hurt kids."

The knife slid across Jennifer's throat, and her eyes grew wide as blood shot out and covered her legs. Her eyes closed. Delia wiped off the knife and placed it back in her sheath. She reached into Jennifer's jacket pocket and pulled out her phone and the new passport and driver's license. She would make sure that Hamza got them both and the pictures of the two men Jennifer had done business with. She stood, picked up the black duffel and tossed it behind a dumpster. She looked at Jennifer and slipped into the shadows. She had two things left to do.

***

Delia stood at the floor-to-ceiling window in the sterile room and looked out over the rain-soaked streets. Her reflection showed a woman physically intact but mentally exhausted. She couldn't remember the last time she'd slept or ate.

She scrolled through Harper's findings on the tablet, examining the evidence of the fabricated intelligence. Her jaw clenched as she considered the implications. Harper had discovered that the Organization had been behind everything. All the bad intel and all the parties who were double- and triple-crossed.

He found out that Delia was pulled into the game in an attempt by the Organization to draw her out of hiding, expose her and eliminate her. Yet with everything that happened, there was no indication that they had any idea she was in Istanbul or how much she had been involved in destroying their plans.

They lost out on getting their hands on the fighter plans, and they lost one of their agents.

Delia placed both palms flat on the cool glass, steadying herself against the wave of disillusionment that threatened to overwhelm her. The horizon stretched out, vast and uncertain, mirroring her thoughts.

The data on the tablet glared back at her, a digital accusation that left no room for denial. They had orchestrated the mission with surgical precision hoping that she would show up. That thought made her smile.

A noise in the background made her turn as the blood pressure cuff inflated automatically. David was lying in the bed, a tube down his throat to help him breathe, a tangle of wires leading to various machines. Red lines blinked, and digital numbers appeared and disappeared.

The doctor told her the surgery had gone well. They had to remove his spleen and replace a piece of an artery, but he expected him to make a full recovery.

Delia sat on the bed, reached out and touched his hand. She had so many questions about his involvement with the Organization, and she questioned if the thirteen years of their marriage were just a scam, a cover meant to keep her in line. She stroked his hand. She had always felt bad because of the lies she had used in their marriage. She thought she was protecting him, but that was not the case.

She leaned closer to his ear. "I always loved you, and I always will," she whispered. His eyelids flickered, and a slit appeared before they closed tight. She kissed him on the forehead, stood and left the room.

Delia took the elevator two flights down and pushed open another door to another sterile room. James Morrison was awake, lying back in the hospital bed, looking at the ceiling. He looked over when the door opened and smiled.

"Delia," he said, his voice raspy after the surgery. Delia stepped up to the bed and pushed on his shoulder as he tried to move.

"Stay," she said, and he stopped moving. "I just stopped by to tell you that Tommy is safe," she said. "The embassy has him staying in one of the visitor's rooms, and they've assigned a full-time caregiver to be with him until you are recovered enough to take him home."

Morrison smiled.

"I've spoken with the Turkish authorities, and you have been cleared of any wrongdoing. They understand you were a pawn and were doing what a father would do in your circumstances."

"What about Jennifer?" he asked. "She hasn't been to see me."

"Jennifer is gone. Her involvement in this whole sordid affair is still being reviewed."

Delia placed the tablet she had gotten from Harper on the table next to the bed. She tapped it with her finger. "When you feel up to it, everything you need to know is on here." She stood and moved to the foot of the bed. "Be well, James Morrison."

Before he could answer, Delia slipped out and was gone.

Delia walked out of the hospital and zipped up her jacket against the wet chill. She flagged down a taxi and gave him the address. She sat back, and her thoughts turned to the Organization and the fact that they tried to manipulate her out into the open. She thought about the entire operation. Were they part of the deception? The suspense tormented her.

Delia thought about David and what part he'd played in the deception. Had he known that they were trying to expose her, or was he just another player in this sick game? The thought left her breathless, the sheer scale of it crashing over her like a rogue wave. She tried to piece together the fragments, to find a pattern in the chaos that surrounded her.

She looked out the window, the streets of Istanbul a blur in her peripheral vision. Her breathing came fast and shallow, her proficient control unraveling as she faced the magnitude of her situation. The suspicion that had taken root now spread, branching out into every corner of her thoughts.

Her instincts screamed at her, the internal alarms blaring with a ferocity she hadn't felt in months. She could see where the danger lay but couldn't pinpoint the source of the threat. She willed herself to focus, to push past the fog of doubt that clouded her vision. The familiar discipline returned, a thin but vital thread she clung to with all her might.

Her world had narrowed to a single point of focus, the betrayal more personal and more dangerous than any she'd faced before. The stakes were higher, the implications more profound. She opened her eyes, the revelation setting in as she made sense of the chaos. Delia wouldn't let it destroy her. Not this time. She took a breath, deep and calming, the air like a balm against the rawness inside.

Her spine straightened, her decision crystallizing in the clarity of the moment. Delia wouldn't run. She wouldn't hide. She would find out what the Organization wanted, find out who had tried to set her up and make them pay.

The reflection in the glass was different now, the uncertainty replaced by something sharper, more focused. The light was still shattered by the raindrops on the window, but she welcomed it, letting it illuminate the path she would take. Delia was a force, a relentless certainty that nothing could stop. She forged ahead, a promise to herself and a threat to whomever dared to cross her.

The sun broke through the clouds, casting the city in brilliance as Delia walked towards her plane, her shadow long and defiant.

Epilogue: Shadows Remain

Delia leaned back on her towel, the sand like a forgotten warmth against her skin. The sky turned vivid with the sun's last colors, oranges and pinks bleeding into each other as if time itself were painting over the day. Her tanned skin glowed against the tiny white bikini. She was a vision of loveliness, a goddess. She took a deep breath of the salty air and held it. She exhaled, felt the calm wrap around her, the sound of the waves like a lullaby that knew nothing of her past.

She looked out over the ocean, each wave a quiet reflection of the chaos she'd left behind. The gentle rustling of the palm fronds, the low murmur of the creatures who inhabited the world around her, even the light—it all spoke of a world in which she belonged. She settled back on the blanket, allowing peace to press in around her.

Her setup was simple, stripped down to the essentials the way she'd trained herself. A towel on the sand, a half-empty glass of wine and a small token of the past: a Turkish coin. It was placed with care, its presence a quiet acknowledgment of where she'd come from and where she might be going. She picked up the glass, took a slow sip and let the warmth travel through her, unwinding every muscle and every thought.

The ocean continued its eternal song, a melody of innocence and forgetting. For once, Delia didn't fight it. She let the waves, the light, all of it wash over her, pulling her further away from who she used to be.

The day slid towards darkness, each moment a sandcastle washed away by the tide of time. Delia heard it, the low chime a specter of urgency. Her phone, a ghost from a life she meant to bury. The call was encrypted, unsettling, as it demanded her focus. New threats. Unresolved threads. Her muscles tightened. She picked up her phone, her eyes pulling towards the ocean as if it might show her a path. But the water had no answers.

She noted the number and answered the call. "Hamza," she said.

"Good evening, Delia," he said. "I hope you had a pleasant flight back to paradise, wherever that might be."

"It's good to be home," she said.

"I wanted to let you know that the hospital expects to release David in a couple of days. We will not bother him, as I expect you might have some unfinished business with your former employer. I will leave that to you. Morrison will return to the embassy tomorrow to be with his son. I have it on good authority that he will have no issues upon his return."

"What happened with the Iranians?" she asked.

"Funny you should ask," he said. "They have reached out to my government and want to continue the economic and security talks. They seem very interested in coming to an agreement."

"That's wonderful," said Delia. "I have one favor to ask. I never got the chance to reach out to Kemal and thank him for the warm reception he arranged for me at the club that night. I was wondering..."

Hamza laughed. "It's so tragic, but I heard Kemal had a terrible accident just yesterday. It seemed he was taking a bath, and a radio fell into the tub, and he was electrocuted. Tragic."

Delia smiled. "Thanks," she said.

"It was my pleasure. Until we meet again."

The call disconnected, and Delia placed the phone on the blanket next to her.

The ocean met her gaze with indifference, its surface smooth and dark. She searched the horizon, the narrowing line between water and sky echoing the narrowing distance between peace and purpose. Retirement or mission. Every consideration was laid bare, her thoughts assembling and reassembling the options with tactical precision. She knew how to weigh risk against reward, how to plan for any outcome. But this was different. The risks were personal, the cost one she'd forgotten how to pay.

Her eyes followed the endless waves, each one a suggestion, a possibility, an unresolved thread. Delia understood the choice like she did the sand beneath her: shifting and elusive, promising nothing. Her mind forged ahead, mapping out the effects of her decision, even as her heart urged her towards the inevitability of action.

Her fingers moved absently in the sand, drawing the outlines of her thoughts. Each pattern was a decision tree, each erased line a doubt discarded. It was as if her body worked through the process before her mind could catch up, a manifestation of the conflict that had already taken root.

The tide claimed the shapes she formed, the grains scattering and regrouping, like plans and plots that refused to stay erased. The tranquility of the beach faded, replaced by the tension of a choice that grew more inevitable with every moment.

Delia perceived the risks, felt them as surely as the wind lifting her hair, the phone had pulled her back. But the pull of the assignment, of unfinished business, was stronger than she'd allowed herself to admit. Stronger than peace, stronger than any promise of freedom.

The water continued its rhythmic assault, relentless and unconcerned. Her past and her future collided on its surface, forming and re-forming as the waves rolled in. And Delia sat with it, letting the decision settle above her like the first stars blinking into the evening sky.

Night draped itself across the beach. Delia finished her wine. She picked up the phone, her thumb hesitating a hair's breadth from the contact on the screen before pressing with conviction. She stood, the connection crackling like electricity in the cooling air. Her silhouette was an ink stain against the last light of sunset, a mark of certainty.

"It's me," she said. "I'm ready."

Stars flickered on, the ocean's voice gaining strength as the world fell still. Lights appeared, constellations on land that seemed to mirror those above. Delia let them guide her.

The breeze lifted strands of her hair, carrying the salt and the chill as it swept over the beach. Her focus narrowed to a single point, a single call that meant leaving behind everything she'd thought she wanted. Her past had found her in paradise, its grip as unyielding as ever. But now Delia met it with equal strength. The name had felt like a question days before, but it came easily now. Familiar, like an old scar.

She held the phone with confidence. She didn't run from her nature, the sense of action settling into her bones like muscle memory. Her retreat had been brief but enough to see the truth she'd hidden from herself. It was not the peace she needed; it was the mission, the purpose, the promise of something unfinished waiting to be completed. Delia's decision was a splinter, sharp and undeniable, impossible to ignore. She pressed her thumb tighter, the ocean's roar and her own heartbeat the reply to her declaration.

Delia took a breath, letting the ocean's rhythm sync with her own. The world shifted into focus, everything sharper, clearer, now that she knew where she was going. What she was leaving behind. Her clothes caught the breeze, the light fabric snapping like flags in a wind that she could feel. She didn't wait for a reply. The answer was already there, beneath the surface, like so many of the truths she carried.

The night took over like a blanket that covered the beach with new possibilities. The lights from other beachfront properties flickered on, pale imitations of stars that stretched all the way to the horizon. Delia welcomed them, letting them show her the way to go. She didn't shy from it. Not this time. She stood against the evening and the past, the call completed, the commitment made. When the next call came, she would be ready.

Acknowledgments

A special thank-you to my daughter Christina J. Morgan, my unofficial collaborator.

Thanks to my editor, Laura Dragonette, whose efforts helped turn my manuscript into a polished novel. Her help is greatly appreciated. Any mistakes the reader may find are solely the responsibility of the author.

Also, I would like to thank my family for their encouragement. I have been telling them stories since they were little, and I always told them that someone should be writing this stuff down. I decided to write it down myself.

A special thanks to my late wife, Jane. She pushed me for years to become a writer, and my biggest regret is that she didn't live long enough to see it happen. I love her with all my heart and miss her every day. I think she would be pleased.

Thanks to the readers. Without you, none of this would be important.

About the Author

2019 Pacific Book Awards Best Mystery Finalist . . . *Crime Delayed*

2020 Pacific Book Awards Best Mystery Winner . . . *Crime Denied*

2020 Chanticleer International Book Awards: 1st Place Blue Ribbon, CLUE Book Awards for Suspense, Thriller Fiction . . . *Crime Denied*

2021 Chanticleer International Book Awards Finalist, CLUE Book Awards for Suspense, Thriller Fiction . . . *Crime Conspiracy*

2021 Chanticleer International Book Awards Finalist, Book Series, CLUE Book Awards for Suspense, Thriller Fiction . . . Crime Series, The Buck Taylor Novels

2022 Chanticleer International Book Awards Finalist, CLUE Book Awards for Suspense, Thriller Fiction . . . *Crime Exploded*

2022 Chanticleer International Book Awards Finalist, CLUE Book Awards for Suspense, Thriller Fiction . . . *Crime Spree*

2023 Chanticleer International Book Awards Finalist, CLUE Book Awards for Suspense, Thriller Fiction . . . *Crime Scene*

2023 Chanticleer International Book Awards Series Finalist, Mystery & Mayhem Book Awards . . . Crime Series

Chuck Morgan attended Seton Hall University and Regis College and spent thirty-five years as a construction project manager. He is an avid outdoorsman, an Eagle Scout and a licensed private pilot. He enjoys camping, hiking, mountain biking and fly-fishing.

He is the author of the Crime series, featuring Colorado Bureau of Investigation Agent Buck Taylor. The series includes *Crime Interrupted, Crime Delayed, Crime Unsolved, Crime Exposed, Crime Denied, Crime Conspiracy, Crime Unknown, Crime Exploded, Crime Spree, Crime Family, Crime Scene, Crime Victims, Crime Unraveled* and *Cold Justice*.

He is also the author of *Her Name Was Jane*, a memoir about his late wife's nine-year battle with breast cancer. He has three children and four grandchildren. He resides in Lone Tree, Colorado.

Other Books by the Author

Dear Reader, thank you for reading this novel. Please enjoy my other series and follow Colorado Bureau of Investigation Agent Buck Taylor and his team as they investigate new and sometimes unusual crimes in the Colorado mountains. Each novel is a separate story, and they can be read in any order, but you might find it more enjoyable to read them in order.

Happy Reading,
Chuck Morgan

"Crime Interrupted: A Buck Taylor Novel by Chuck Morgan is a gripping, edge-of-the-seat novel. Right from page one, the action kicks off and never stops, gaining pace as each chapter passes." Reviewed by Anne-Marie Reynolds for Readers' Favorite.*

Finalist . . . 2019 Pacific Book Awards Best Mystery
*"**This crime novel reads like a great thriller.** The writing is atmospheric, laced with vivid descriptions that capture the setting in great detail while allowing readers to follow the intensity of the action and the emotional and psychological depth of the story." Reviewed by Divine Zape for Readers' Favorite.*

*"**Professionally written in the style of a best-selling crime novelist, such as Tom Clancy, Crime Unsolved: A Buck Taylor Novel by Chuck Morgan is a spellbinding suspense novel with an environmental flair.** Intriguing subplots of fraud, survivalist paranoia, and murder weave their way through the fabric of the plot, creating a dynamic story. This is an action-filled, stimulating tale which contains fascinating details that are relevant in our present climate." Reviewed by Susan Sewell for Readers' Favorite.*

"Chuck Morgan has a unique gift for plot, one that makes Crime Exposed: A Buck Taylor Novel a hard-to-put-down book. *From the start, readers know what happens to Barb, but they become curious as they follow the investigation, wondering if the characters will find out what happened to her. The descriptions are filled with clarity, and they offer readers great images. The prose is elegant, and it captures both the emotional and psychological elements of the novel clearly while offering vivid descriptions of scenes and characters. This is a fast-paced thriller with memorable characters and a criminal investigation that is so real readers will believe it could happen." Reviewed by Romuald Dzemo for Readers' Favorite.*

Winner . . . 2020 Pacific Book Awards Best Mystery

2020 Chanticleer International Book Awards: 1st Place Blue Ribbon, CLUE Book Awards for Suspense, Thriller Fiction

"It's really progressive to see a female serial killer portrayed with such intelligent writing and depth of character, *and the cat and mouse chase dynamic is thrown off nicely by the switching of genders. What results is a really enjoyable thriller and crime mystery novel, and overall Crime Denied is certain to please fans of both hard-boiled detective tales* *and action/adventure crime novels.*" Reviewed by K.C. Finn for Readers' Favorite.

2021 Chanticleer International Book Awards Finalist, CLUE Book Awards for Suspense, Thriller Fiction . . . *Crime Conspiracy*

"This makes for a truly dynamic story where anything is possible, and a hero you can root for even when it looks like all is lost." Reviewed by K.C. Finn for Readers' Favorite.

"This is a book you can't put down, which will entertain you on many levels, and at times make your skin crawl; the kind of book that remains in your thoughts long after you finish reading." Reviewed by Steven Robson for Readers' Favorite.

"I read Crime Unknown in one sitting. The plot is intense and the main character, Agent Buck Taylor, is a hero like no other. This book has everything a thriller needs to be and more. I thought I knew the story at the beginning. Buck will solve a tricky murder case, I thought. But Chuck Morgan adds a twist to this story that expands it and makes it one of the most enjoyable books I've read in this genre. I loved that the lead was such an awesome well-rounded fellow but that he also had a support team who were just as important to the story." Reviewed by Maureen Dangarembizi for Readers' Favorite.

"Crime Unknown is a thoroughly enjoyable read and I would not hesitate to recommend this book to fans of the crime genre and those looking for a gateway in." Reviewed by K.C. Finn for Readers' Favorite.

2022 Chanticleer International Book Awards Finalist, CLUE Book Awards for Suspense, Thriller Fiction . . . *Crime Exploded*

"Action-packed and fast-paced, I was sucked into the story the moment I opened the novel. The author built the story to perfection. Chuck Morgan gave just the right amount of suspense, mystery, and action to keep readers' attention on Buck and his

team. There was never a dull moment in the story. The narrative ran smoothly until the end; it followed the development of the story and the pace set by the characters. I enjoyed the twists and turns. What I loved more than anything else in the plot was how calculating Buck was. He was smart; he didn't let the FBI discourage him and kept his head in the game. The action gave me an adrenaline rush. Absolutely brilliant!" Reviewed by Rabia Tanveer for Readers' Favorite.

2022 Chanticleer International Book Awards Finalist, CLUE Book Awards for Suspense, Thriller Fiction . . . *Crime Spree*

"It is one of the best crime novels I have read in a long while, with real characters developed in a way to let you get to know them intimately, understand them, and appreciate their strengths and weaknesses. *The plot is tight, exciting, and tense, with plenty of action, and it will grip you from the start. The bizarre storyline is enthralling, written in descriptive prose that lands you right in the middle of the action. Forget sleep; once you pick this book up, you won't want to put it down until it's finished. Fantastic story, and highly recommended for fans of high-octane crime thrillers." Reviewed by Anne-Marie Reynolds for Readers' Favorite.*

*"**Crime Family is the tenth book in the Buck Taylor series. Chuck Morgan had me hooked from the first page until the end.** There was never a dull moment with all the action; one chapter flowed into the next. The story was fast-paced and kept me on the edge of my seat. I kept turning the pages to find out what would happen next. I was intrigued, and with all the twists and turns, I could not predict what was looming. The characters were well-developed. Each had a background description, and it was fun getting to know some of them. The story was excellently written with a fitting ending." Reviewed by Alma Boucher for Readers' Favorite.*

*"**Crime Scene is a must-read for lovers of mystery sleuth and murder tales with a touch of conspiracy.**" Readers' Favorite review.*

"Crime Scene has a carefully designed intrigue that deepens with every unforeseeable turn of events and a dynamic narrative." Readers' Favorite review.

"This is a great book. Holds your attention and you don't want to put it down. I would recommend this book to anyone who loves a good crime novel." Amazon review.

"Spellbinding, gripping, powerful, and relevant are just a few words that come to mind after turning the last page of Crime Scene: A Buck Taylor Novel, Book 11, by Chuck Morgan." Amazon Review.

"A riveting plot and good pacing keep the reader in suspense as Buck Taylor and his team establish evidence beyond a reasonable doubt. The author sustains interest by skillfully showing the art and intuition involved in crime investigation and the science behind it, as well as the elements that can delay or confound it. There are a lot of quirky characters in the novel and the author gives them mannerisms, voices and descriptions that make them distinctive and realistic. The details and descriptions of the work and everyday life of the players are both pleasantly appealing and revolting, depending on the scenario. What's most captivating and intriguing about the character development is the backstory of the unhinged characters and how the author uses them as part of the perplexing trail of

a horrendous crime. Themes of sadism, cruelty, grief, forensics, police procedures, and even a little bit of romance can be found in this installment of the Buck Taylor series. Highly recommended for crime story fans who especially enjoy the information as well as the twists, turns, and the untangling of intricate and cold case crime sprees." Reviewed by Carmen Tenorio for Readers' Favorite.

◇◇◇◇◇*"Resurrection by Chuck Morgan presents a riveting, suspense-filled story involving the Nazis and a plan to gain power in modern-day New York. It's 2024, and the Nazis are back with vengeance." Readers' Favorite review.*

◇◇◇◇◇*"If you're a fan of thrillers and history, get this book today!" Readers' Favorite review.*

◇◇◇◇◇*"Chuck Morgan has penned a unique, fascinating story with sharp, believable dialogue that perfectly drives the plot forward. The pacing is impressive and immersive." Readers' Favorite review.*

◇◇◇◇◇ *"This is a literary masterpiece that would make an intriguing movie. Bravo to Mr. Morgan for writing a story examining the "what if" element that reflects on the impact of history in today's world." Readers' Favorite review.*